SUMMER IN THE HOUSE OF THE DEPARTED

Josh Rountree

PSYCHOPOMP

SUMMER IN THE HOUSE OF THE DEPARTED

© 2025 Josh Rountree
All Rights Reserved.

ISBN-13: 979-8-89116-013-2

Published by Psychopomp
psychopomp.com

Publisher's Note:
No part of this publication may be reproduced, distributed, or transmitted in any form or by any means, including photocopying, recording, or other electronic or mechanical methods, without the prior written permission of the publisher, except in the case of brief quotations embodied in critical reviews and certain other noncommercial uses permitted by copyright law.

This book is a work of fiction. Names, characters, places, and incidents either are products of the author's imagination or are used fictitiously. Any resemblance to actual persons, living or dead, events, or locales is entirely coincidental.

Cataloging-in-Publication Data
Names: Rountree, Josh, author.
Title: Summer in the House of the Departed
Description: Woodbury, VT : Psychopomp [2025]
Identifiers: ISBN: 9798891160132 (paperback)
Subjects: LCSH: Ghosts—Fiction. |
BISAC: FICTION / Ghost. |

Cover & interior formatted by Christine M. Scott
clevercrow.com

Cover illustration by Inkshark

THIS ONE'S FOR NANNY.
Thanks for all the ghosts.

TABLE OF CONTENTS

O LOST, AND BY THE WIND GRIEVED,
GHOST, COME BACK AGAIN.

- Thomas Wolfe, Look Homeward, Angel

SUMMER 1981

The summer my grandmother disappeared, taking an entire Texas town with her, she showed me photos of her ghosts.

She placed the photos on the kitchen counter, snapping each one against the shell-pink Formica like playing cards. Some of the more interesting ones she tapped with her finger to make sure I took special notice. "That one there was taken out near Sterling City."

"You took it?"

"No, a woman lives there took it. Sent it to me."

It was a Polaroid with *Thanksgiving 1978* written along the bottom. A little girl with a long-sleeve shirt and blue jeans tucked into red cowboy boots sat in a high-backed wicker chair, laughing, and pointing back at the camera. Blue light blossomed out from behind the chair in a vaguely humanoid shape, and two tendrils wrapped around the girl like transparent arms, giving her a hug.

"Lady who sent this says the girl is her daughter, and the ghost is her late mother. She died that summer before. The old woman used to favor that chair. Her ghost started making a whole lot of racket around the house anytime somebody sat in it. This was a few years back, so might be she's moved along by now."

"What kind of racket?"

"Oh, just knocking on walls and stomping around. I recorded it. It's on one of my cassettes."

I wasn't sure I wanted to hear it. The thought of dying and being bound to the real world while everyone carried on around you was more frightening to me than the ghosts themselves. If I had to die, I figured I'd rather go someplace else.

Granny filled an ashtray full of lipstick-stained cigarette butts while we talked our way through her stack of photos. Some she'd taken herself, others she'd received from people familiar with her reputation. Most of the photos showed smiling people with circular splotches above their heads, or streaks of light cutting across the image. Maybe the camera captured a bug. Maybe it was a trick of the light. Others were harder to explain, like the crying woman floating above a glassy lake, draped in a long white dress, arms outstretched.

Granny put down a second photo of the same floating woman, same position, like it was taken immediately after the first, except this time the woman's dress was stained a deep red and she had the head of a horse. Her body was soft around the edges, like the camera had moved before the image could resolve.

"This one shows La Llorona. You remember the story I told you?"

"Yes, I know that one." I stared at the picture. The horse woman's lips were curled back around her flat teeth in a way that made it look like she was smiling.

"Might not ought to show you some of these."

"Why not?"

"They're liable to keep you up with nightmares."

"Can I see the ones they took here?"

"Let's save those for another time."

Various people had taken photos in Granny's house, both before and after she moved here, and she kept them in a cigar box in her desk, stacks of them bound with rubber bands. She'd always been happy to show me the rest of her photo collection, no matter how terrifying, but so far, she'd never been inclined to show me those in the cigar box.

I wasn't sure why she thought they would frighten me more than the others. More than her house itself.

The place was thoroughly haunted.

That's why she'd moved there in the first place.

———

Ghosts bled out from the margins of that old house, and I made friends with a few of them. Like thin gray memories they clung to the undersides of coffee tables and dwelled in the narrow space between the guest bed and the wall. In the nighttime, I'd peer over the edge of the mattress at their dull forms and whisper my secrets to them. They wouldn't respond, but I judged their interest in the way their eyes never wavered from mine.

In the daylight they were like half-erased pencil marks against the windows and the walls, often escaping notice and more easily forgotten, but still grasping at whatever reality they called their own.

Among my favorites was the ghost of a girl about my age whom I'd decided to call Shirley. She wore an old-style dress I couldn't place in time, and she lingered at my grandmother's bookshelves, drawing the outline of her fingertips across the spines of the books. The raspy sound of her fingers running against the paperbacks was the only noise she ever made. When she settled on one,

I'd read it aloud to her. Frequently it would be *We Have Always Lived in the Castle*, but today it was *Something Wicked This Way Comes*, and I believe she picked this one because I'd told her it was my favorite.

We passed most mornings this way, me a pudgy boy in beat-up tennis shoes and brown corduroys, my hair buzzed down in what they used to call a summer cut, and her, little more than a silver outline of the person she used to be, but with blue eyes that had never entirely released their hold on life.

My grandmother often watched us from the doorway; Granny was wraith-thin and hollowed by cancer, a wreath of cigarette smoke spinning over her head. She was only in her mid-fifties, which seemed appropriately old for a grandparent when I was eight, but shockingly young now that I'm chasing that age myself.

One morning, my grandmother's research assistant arrived wearing loose jeans and a blouse, lugging a legal box full of paperwork, blonde hair knotted up on top of her head and sunglasses sliding down the end of her nose. Beverly was an English major at Angelo State with an eye toward folklore and the supernatural, and her whirlwind arrival blew the ghosts to hidden corners of the house. I'd learned the summer before that despite her interest in ghosts, Beverly couldn't see the ones living here. She struck me as too energetic, too *alive* for the ghosts to reveal themselves.

I wasn't sure what that said about me.

"Hey kid, what are you reading?" Beverly sat the box on the table and gave me a hug. I showed her the paperback in my hand. "I like that one," she said. "But I like his science fiction stuff better."

My grandmother greeted Beverly wearing an orange polyester pantsuit and the wig she wore whenever we left the house, or when company called. She dug through the papers Beverly had brought, turquoise bracelets clattering together on her wrists. She clenched a lit cigarette between her teeth when she spoke. "Any accounts here from primary sources?"

Beverly settled into a chair at the dining room table, where my grandmother had already spilled the paperwork across the surface in untidy stacks. "Not much. Nothing that would be new to you, anyway. But there's some good general info about the time period, and a lot of quotable speculation over the years of what CROATOAN might mean."

"Thank you, honey. Looks like some good stuff."

"I also found some stories I don't think you've referenced yet that might add color and corroboration. Small towns in California and Ohio that disappeared around the turn of the century. And this one here in Kansas, back in the fifties."

Beverly slid a paper-clipped bundle of materials toward my grandmother.

"You're talking about Ashley, Kansas?"

"Yes. Earthquake, fire from the sky. A lot of creepy calls to the cops about the dead coming back for a visit. And then everybody in the whole town just disappeared. There are a couple of phone numbers written down there. People who lived nearby when it happened. I got a hold of them, and they're willing to talk to you."

"This is good work. I've heard that story before, but nothing as detailed as this."

"There's talk of a hole in the sky," said Beverly. "Maybe it connects to another dimension? That supports a scientific answer to this mystery, don't you think?"

"Might be it does," said my grandmother. "Either way, it's interesting."

I huddled underneath the table like one of the ghosts, hungry for scraps. I often learned more about what Beverly and my grandmother were researching when they forgot I was there. Shirley attached herself to the underside of the table too, a swirling mass with shining eyes, head cocked to the side like she was listening. We lazed there together, lulled half asleep by the heat and their voices.

"Another universe bumping up against this one is the only rational explanation, isn't it?" Beverly took a seat at the table and tapped her shoe nervously against the floorboards. Shirley drifted close, grasped at the cuff of Beverly's blue jeans with smoky fingers. Shirley had that dusty, moldering smell that many of us associate with long afternoons spent digging through forgotten bookstores, and I would carry that with me through life as the scent of my grandmother's house.

"Why do you assume there's a rational explanation?" my grandmother asked.

"There has to be, right?"

"There has to be an explanation," my grandmother said, "but no reason it has to be rational."

Granny wrote nonfiction books about the supernatural, and her latest project was about the Roanoke colony. I'd read about what happened there. As soon as I was old enough to sound out words, my grandmother loaded me down with books about aliens, bigfoot, ghosts, trolls living under bridges, portals to fairy kingdoms, doomsday cults, and by comparison, more prosaic mysteries like the story of Roanoke. I knew Roanoke was a colony of early American settlers who had disappeared in the late fifteen hundreds, leaving no clue to where they'd gone, except the word CROATOAN cut into the bark of a tree. Most historians figured they'd either been killed by natives or assimilated into one of their tribes, but such an enduring mystery was bound to elicit supernatural speculation as well.

I peered out from underneath the table, spying on them like another forgotten ghost.

"If you throw out science, how can you hope to figure all this out?" said Beverly. "That's crazy, right?"

Before Granny moved here, before she got *sick*, she taught high school. English 101. Both levels of Spanish. She was accustomed to questions and reveled in learning. So, she accepted Beverly's challenge in the spirit it was intended.

Granny smiled, struggled with the striker on her lighter as she started another cigarette.

"I don't throw out science, honey," she said. "And I don't doubt there's some *rational* outcome for what's going on that you'd accept in those terms, if you had a textbook in your hands that codified it. But that won't ever happen. Science won't provide you that answer. You know why? Science is too *proud*. Science won't dig deep enough. I've read reams of evidence on the supernatural, including your good work here. Testimonials by credible folks with no reason to lie. Photos. Recordings. Objectively provable psychic phenomena. Do scientists consider these things? Not many of them. Not if they value their reputation. No quicker way to get shunned by academia than admit you believe in ghosts and goblins. And that's a shame. Because science is supposed to consider *all* evidence, isn't it? How accurate can your finding be on a matter if you pretend a good bulk of evidence just doesn't exist?"

"I don't know," said Beverly.

"Well, they don't either. What I'm saying, girl, is all that stuff we call the supernatural is a *natural* part of science. You just can't study it under a microscope or swirl it around in a test tube."

"You know I love folklore," said Beverly. "*Stories*. But there must be some real-world answer for these sorts of disappearances, right? These people aren't being stolen away by fairies."

"You're sure of that?"

Beverly grinned, chewed at her bottom lip as she tried to figure out if Granny was joking. Tried to ready some sort of logical argument if she wasn't. The genuine delight on her face, and the way she drew her hair back through her fingers when she was thinking intently, made something flutter in my stomach. She smelled like coconut shampoo and sunshine. Like she lived on a tropical beach and not in the same forsaken land as the rest of us. Beverly belonged someplace else. Someplace better. She was beautiful, and I suppose I had a crush on her, but my eight-year-old self wouldn't have understood it in those terms.

"You know I've experienced things too?" said Granny. "Not to mention there's ghosts all over this house. Brady here sees them. Don't you?"

Blood rushed to my face, and I nodded. Beverly gave me an appraising look, like she wasn't sure what planet I'd materialized from.

"You've told me all the stories, Mrs. Edwards."

"They're more than *stories*," said Granny.

"Sorry, that's not what I meant. I believe all this stuff is happening, but there's just..." Beverly trailed off, absently flipped through a few of the pages on the tabletop, as if the secrets of the universe might suddenly reveal themselves.

"Uh huh," said Granny. "That's where we get caught up, isn't it? *Just*. That's where our strictly materialist view of the universe falls apart."

"I just need something to hold on to," said Beverly.

"That's the trick, ain't it?"

Shirley drifted from underneath the table like silver smoke, her swirling surface capturing sunlight from another world. Her smile was mischief, and her eyes burned blue. She wanted me to follow. Shirley was restless; she never liked to remain in one place for long unless she was listening to me read. Books always calmed her. Rooted her in the world. I was the same way. I could burn away long hours without moving, so long as there were other places for me to visit in the pages of a book.

Never squirming, never impatient.

Other places always seemed better than wherever I was.

The flavor of conversation between Granny and Beverly was the same as always, so when Shirley issued the call to adventure, I followed. Crawled on all fours like a coyote sniffing at her trail. She moved across the kitchen linoleum like fog creeping across the face of the world, escaped the room and advanced down the hallway. Moving, eventually, under the closed door that led into Granny's den. My bare hands and feet slapped against the floorboards as I followed. The wood was stained with something dark, and smelled like animals had lived here long ago.

A ghost I'd named Glen waited at the doorway. Might be he was standing guard, but I couldn't know his motives. I wasn't allowed in Granny's den alone. But I was determined to follow Shirley, find out what she was up to. Glen was the ghost of an old cowboy with a crushed and weathered hat; he was nothing but bones inside his musty suit. Sometimes he wore a drawn, fretful face, wrinkled and ashen, but today he revealed only his gray, pitted skull, half his teeth fallen out and cracks radiating out from one eye socket like rays from the noonday sun. Shadows ruled the hallway, and he drew form from the darkness, appearing almost substantial. His jaw opened and closed with a sound like a cinder block dragging over concrete. Whatever he wanted to say, I wasn't listening. I reached through him, turned the glass-handled doorknob, and proceeded into the den.

The room Granny called her *den* was a study, just off the hallway near the front entrance to the house. A cracked brick fireplace dominated one wall, mouth black and choking out the old scent of mesquite ash. Bookshelves crowded the other walls, overflowing with titles like *The Kybalion. The Secret Teachings of All Ages. The Book of Lies.* All manner of seductive-sounding volumes that drew my young self in like bugs to the porch lights. I had free run of Granny's bookshelves, apart from those in her den. I would not read these books until much later, when I was older, and seeking insight into my grandmother's thinking, there at the end of her life. I can't say it made much of a difference.

Questing for any true answer was folly, though it took me decades to learn that.

Stuffed in with the books were file folders and yellow notebooks full of Granny's neat handwriting. Stacks of generic white cassette tapes with labels like *Little Girl Ghost, Jumping on Bed. Snyder, TX 1972* and *Interview #2 with Mrs. Mabel Starch / Plainview Prairie Beast Encounter.* Melted candles and grinning crystal skulls. Wooden boxes carved with smiling suns and sleeping moons. Shirley rested a hand on top of one of those boxes, smiling dreamily. Her intention clear. Summer sunlight tried to intrude through the room's lone window, but tan lace curtains and layers of West Texas dust held it at bay. What light existed in the room was golden and soft. *Ghost light.* Perfect shading for Shirley to take form. Unseen winds pulled at her calico dress. Her fingers clutched at the box, like she was trying to lift it herself. I didn't question her. I met her hopeful stare and nodded. Snatched the box from the shelf and held it in my tiny hands.

I climbed into the swivel chair at Granny's big oak desk, sat the box on top, careful not to disturb anything. Not to leave evidence of my *trespass.* The desk was littered with scraps of paper, mostly letters from people who sought out my grandmother for her advice on the supernatural. A few photos lay scattered about. Blurry images of supposed ghosts, and one that looked like a canine jowl streaking red through thick sagebrush. That one was paper clipped to a handwritten note claiming an encounter with the Chupacabra.

Normally these photos would have drawn me in; they weren't among those Granny had shown me before. But the wooden box held the promise of unknown treasure, and Shirley clung cold against my back, obviously eager for me to open it. When I did, I found more photos. A couple dozen of them, bound in a fat rubber band. Every one of them taken inside Granny's house. I heard that cinder-block scrape again, and realized Glen had joined us. He stood right behind me, snared by the same curiosity that held Shirley. The same curiosity that held me.

I fumbled off the rubber band. Laid the photos out.

The shooting locations were instantly recognizable. Granny's upstairs bedroom. The kitchen, in the corner where the wobbly breakfast table stood. The formal living room, in front of the great brick fireplace. Even a few in the bathroom. Every photo taken right here in Granny's house; every photo filled with ghostly apparitions. None of the ghosts appeared on film as clearly as they did to my waking eyes, but a few were substantial enough that I recognized them as my friends. One photo captured the old woman I'd named Lady Pecan Tree, standing beside the bed in my room, staring out the dormer window as was her habit. Blue and shimmery and transparent. Another photo showed Glen in the front living room, worn hat tipped forward to cover most of his missing face. Ephemeral hands locked together in worry. I kept flipping through the photos, found one of myself, very much alive, standing in front the towering bookshelves in the library. Some of the photos were older, but Granny took this one. Shirley stood beside me, both of us staring at the camera, like we were posing together. And I suppose we were. Shirley and I were fast friends, no matter the distance that separated us. No matter how much she wished me dead, so we might play and read together for eternity.

The ghosts at my back remained cold and still.

None of these photos were remotely frightening, and as I continued to examine them, I wondered why Granny held this particular batch in reserve.

Then I came to the last photo in the pile.

It was taken in the entryway, the camera eye facing the front door. A stained glass window dominated the top half of the door; it showed a stylized reproduction of an old-time cattle drive, beeves lumbering across the vanished prairie, cowboys on horseback, herding them ever onward. Sunlight stampeded through the glass, spilling reds and greens and golds across the floor and the walls. Bathed in that sunlight was the ghost of a man, arms crossed and grinning. So striking was the image, that if not for the way the sunlight passed through him, I might have mistaken him for a visitor to the house, waiting by the door to leave. He wore a pair of green coveralls, pants legs tucked into tall boots. His gray hair was thin and neatly combed, and a few days' worth of stubble grew on his chin. His green eyes shone with otherworldly light. They stared at the camera. Stared at the photographer. Stared at *me*.

It was my grandfather.

Five years dead.

Granny, it seemed, had good reason for her secrets.

Granny's house was a two-story Victorian with a wraparound porch, built by some bygone cattle rancher when this country was still wild. It stood tall and imposing, leaning ever so slightly eastward, a concession to a century of relentless wind. Deep in the nights, I could hear that wind screaming against the window glass, like an animal in pain. The house would shake and rattle, but never gave in. Beyond the town were lonely miles of farmland, cut through with barbwire fences. Populated with chugging green tractors, rusted troughs, and cattle gates locked tight with heavy chains. Houses and barns lay scattered amid fields of cotton, white buds beginning to peek out from the sea of green. Heat rippled up from the earth, and carried with it the pervasive smell of manure.

I loved the *expansiveness* of the place. Nothing like the Dallas suburbs. At home, I was penned in. Always kept busy by whatever my parents believed I should be doing. But at Granny's house, half a state away and at the very edge of the world, summer unwound at a leisurely pace, and my activities were mine to choose. Though I spent most of my time in the cool indoors, I'd stare out across the town from the window in my bedroom, beyond the two-lane highway that navigated the horizon, and into the hazy blue distance. Standing before that window gave me an intense sort of vertigo, like all that empty space needed to be *filled*. Like the land itself might suck me through the beveled glass and carry me away. I'd breathe it all in. Heart thundering. I'd delight in the heady feeling of falling forward. And I'd dream of a comfortable forever spent in that house, in that place, far from the chaos of home.

Granny liked spending time on her covered porch, where she could watch the comings and goings of the two hundred-odd souls who lived in the town. We'd go out there early each morning with our mugs of coffee; hers was black and steaming, mine mostly milk, with a couple of saccharin tablets tossed in. We'd sit and talk until the heat chased us inside. In the evenings, when the sun finally lowered itself behind the towering bulk of the old Baptist church, we'd return to the porch. She lived a block off the town square, and though most of the buildings would be dark by then, the combination gas station and café would still be serving, and the golden glow from their windows looked like the last light in the universe.

"Have I told you the story about the rock house?"

She had, the summer before. But I liked hearing her stories, so I shook my head. Told her I hadn't. It was close to ten o'clock, pure dark, but bedtimes didn't concern Granny. She loved sharing stories as much as I loved hearing them. And looking back, I believe she revealed more of her truths in the black heart of night than she ever dared during daylight.

"Well, there's a house out near Paint Rock. Built of yellow river rock in the 1880s. It stands not a hundred yards from Kickapoo Creek. Legend says nobody knows who built it, but cowboys used to pass through that way and stop by, and they'd always find a hot meal on the table. The house was lived-in, well-kept, but was always empty. Nobody knew who prepared the meals. It was all pretty unsettling, I imagine, but a free meal is a free meal. Well, in the forties some folks from Ireland bought the land, moved in, and made it their home. They were farmers, and by all accounts, upstanding members of the community. One day, some friends from town came to call, and found the house abandoned. Looked like there'd been a slaughter. Blood on the walls and everything. But there was a hot meal on the table, just like always. Roast and potatoes. Hot buttered bread."

"I don't think I'd eat ghost food," I said.

"You're wise to be cautious," she said.

"Tell the rest."

"Thought I hadn't told you this one before."

"Maybe you did. Tell it, though."

"Okay. Their disappearance was a mystery for a while, then there was a big natural gas explosion by the creek. Sent river rocks flying into the air and scattered them all over the prairie. Some of the rocks piled up into a sort of tower, and come to find, none of those rocks were native to Texas. Whole buncha geologists drove up from Houston and they were all baffled. Eventually they determined those rocks were from a certain part of Arizona. Couple of old boys took some samples to Arizona for comparison, and they found the exact spot the rocks came from. You know what else they found?"

I did, but I shook my head.

"They found grave markers," she said. "Three of them. The final resting place of them Irish folks."

"If they died at the rock house, how'd they get there? And did they leave their ghosts behind?"

"Not everything has an easy answer, Brady."

"Maybe I'd eat the ghost food if I could see the ghosts, make sure they're friendly."

"Your eyes can fool you," she said.

"Do you see the ghosts in *this* house?"

"Oh yes," she said. "Maybe not as clear as you do, but I can see them moving in the world."

"They don't scare you?"

"No more than they scare you."

That made me feel good. The fact that Granny understood my bravery. Ghosts might frighten other children, but I felt a kinship to them. Just as my grandmother did. It was something beautiful we shared, and in that moment, I felt an intense love for her. We watched one another for a time, like each was a mystery the other was trying to solve. Wind rattled the shutters and drew screams from the old windmill in the back field. Granny exhaled a cloud of smoke, and the wind stole it away in an instant. My good sentiments fled, replaced suddenly by the terrible thought that Granny might vanish from my life at any moment.

I was old enough to understand how sick she was, if not all the circumstances of the matter. My parents talked. My parents *argued*. And I'd heard enough to know the sort of cancer that killed my grandfather was now taking my grandmother too, and this might be our last summer together.

Tears flooded my eyes, and I felt ashamed of my earlier trespass. "Granny, I went in your den. I looked at all those pictures in the box."

"I know, Brady. I figured you'd fess up."

Granny ashed into the Maxwell House coffee can that sat on the porch railing for just that purpose. She tried and failed to hide her smile.

"How'd you know?" I asked.

"You ain't exactly the CIA."

"Well, I'm sorry."

"No need for sorry," she said. "Boy needs to get up to mischief now and again. I suppose you saw the one with your Grandaddy in it?"

"Yes."

"Let me ask you then. You ever see him around here?"

I shook my head. "No, ma'am."

"That don't surprise me."

"Why?"

"He wouldn't want to scare you."

"Do you see him?" I asked.

"No, I never have," she said.

This evidently pained her. Misery colored her face for a moment, then she turned toward the night, hid it from me. Granny tossed her cigarette butt into the can, pulled a piece of hard peppermint candy from her pocket, and fumbled with the cellophane wrapper. She trembled as she worked at it. Realizing how intently I watched her, she pulled out a second piece, asked if I wanted it.

"No, ma'am."

"My mouth gets dry," she said.

There was nothing to say, so I watched her chew at the candy and light up another cigarette.

"That picture is the reason I moved here," she said.

"Do you think he's here? His ghost, I mean."

"There's no telling, but when I learned about this place, and got my hands on that picture. Well, I was certainly going to find out."

My memories of the house where my grandparents used to live were already fuzzy, as if my eight years on earth were entirely too much to catalog. I recalled brown chickens picking at the weeds, and the family of feral cats who patrolled the barn. Granny cooking liver and onions on a teal stovetop, the salty smell suffusing the air and the clattering of her spatula. This was in a different town—not so far away from where she lived now, but far enough that she'd left all her friends behind when she moved here. Her daughter, my mother, had objected fiercely to the relocation, but she hadn't understood Granny's motivation for the move. None of us had, until now. But if Grandaddy's spirit was here, as it appeared he might be? Well, that's something my mother would never understand, but Granny's reasons were clear as window glass to me.

"Do you think you can bring Grandaddy back?" I immediately regretted the question. It was a stupid notion. But Granny considered it a long time before answering.

"I used to think dead is dead, Brady. But I'm not all that sure now. You've seen all these ghosts around here. I believe there are places in the world, like this one, where the afterlife is so close, you can reach out and touch it."

"Like this house?" I asked.

"Like this *place*. This part of the land. Whatever is happening around here goes back long before this house was built. Best I can figure, when conditions are right, the living and the dead can come together. A person can cross over between here and there. Wherever *there* is. Problem is, I haven't sorted out yet what makes those conditions right."

"Like a portal to heaven or hell?"

"Oh heavens no. There's a whole lot more out there than that. I swear, your parents would have my hide if they knew I was telling you all this."

"The book you're writing," I said. "About Roanoke? Did they disappear from one of these weird places?"

Granny grew suddenly serious, like I'd guessed a secret she wasn't ready to share. She struggled to light a fresh cigarette, but the wind kept stealing away her lighter flame.

"Sometimes I forget how sharp you are, Brady."

"I read a lot of books."

Granny offered a failed smile. "Maybe too many."

"So, is that what happened?"

"No way to know for sure that's where they went, but I believe it's the case. I have some theories I hope are true."

"Well, I wouldn't go there," I said. "If a portal to the dead place opened and they tried to take me, I'd fight back."

"I don't think it's a bad place," she said.

"It's like dying, isn't it?"

"I don't know, Brady. Not exactly, but near enough to it, I suppose. Time may come when you understand better. A person gets older, they can get so tired of living that the prospect of death don't sound like the worst fate in the world. The older you get, the more loneliness comes stalking. And pain with it. The world starts to take things from you that you can never get back, and you might see that portal as someplace where you can start fresh, and track down all you've lost. There's no telling what happened to them Roanoke people, but I like to think they just found someplace they liked better."

That sort of longing wasn't a foreign concept to me, even at such a young age. Books interested me much more than the real world. And the places in those pages called to me. Middle-earth. Melniboné. Bradbury's Green Town. All perilous, but vital and alive in a way reality never could be. Upon closing a book, I often felt a desperate sort of sadness. People carried on their grand adventures in those pages, but I was consigned to the dull and concrete world of warring parents, dying grandmothers, and the approaching end of summer, when school would return, and with it the taunts, the petty violence, the isolation. If there was a portal that could deliver me to the Shire, I'd walk through it willingly. If the hobbits came calling, they could have me without a fight. Granny's description of a world so hard that fleeing it entirely was a desperately desired outcome was closer to my heart than I would have liked. And for the first time, I realized how Granny might be feeling, what things she might be considering.

The prospect of losing her forever cut into my heart and released a flood of sorrow.

Granny had grown thin, her face no more than a skull with pale, transparent skin. A stocking cap covered her bald head, even in the heat. The Adirondack chair she occupied dwarfed her small frame. I scrambled down from my chair, joined Granny in hers, squeezed in beside her and buried my face against her chest so I could feel her heartbeat. Tears burned in my eyes again. When my mother and my grandmother argued, they were always loud, so I knew that Granny had put an end to any treatments, and was prepared to ride out the remainder of her life in this house, with whatever time she was given. I was too young then to recognize words like *mastectomy* and *metastatic*, but I had my own vocabulary for Granny's condition. *Pain, suffering, death.* Now with her talk of fresh starts and tiring of life, I knew she'd plotted a course I couldn't follow. And I realized with a certainty this would be our last summer together.

"Lord, are you crying?" She put an arm around me and squeezed. She smelled like menthol smoke and peppermint.

I shook my head *no*, but of course it was a lie.

"I didn't mean to scare you with all my stories."

"I don't want you to go," I said.

"I ain't going anywhere," she said. "Not right now."

But Granny was lying too, and I knew it.

Everything she yearned for was within her reach.

———————

The next time Beverly came to call, Granny was moving slow, but she straightened her wig, stuffed her beaded cigarette pouch into her purse, and announced she was treating us to lunch at the café. Beverly offered to drive us in her yellow Datsun hatchback, but Granny insisted she needed the exercise, and so at eleven, we left the old house and made the two-block trek to the café in the already torturous summer heat. Untroubled by the temperature, Granny wore a purple satin jacket. Beverly let her set the pace, and I followed in their wake, poking at the ground with a mesquite limb, pausing occasionally to stir up red ant beds in the gravel alongside the road.

It was a Tuesday, and the town was mostly quiet, save for a few men in three-piece suits milling about in front for the courthouse and some children about my age racing bikes through the IGA grocery store parking lot. One boy clipped a shopping cart and set it in motion. The cart cut a slow path across the asphalt, one broken wheel shuddering the whole way, until finally it kissed up against a dirty white pickup truck parked in the shade of a pecan tree. The kids shrieked. Laughed. Made their escape. Battered tennis shoes put pedals into furious motion. Part of me wanted to follow them. To see what sort of trouble we could find. But most of me understood they wouldn't accept me. If I couldn't make friends back home, why should my luck be any different here?

When we arrived at the café, Beverly stepped ahead of Granny to open the door for her. Air-conditioned cold rushed out, invited us in.

"Good morning, Mrs. Edwards. Table for three?"

The hostess was a middle-aged woman with black hair running to gray. Her name tag read MARTA. She produced a businesslike smile and hugged a stack of plastic-covered menus against her chest.

"If you have room. We didn't make a reservation."

Granny smiled. She'd intended her comment as a joke—the lunch rush hadn't started and only a third of the tables were occupied—but Marta gave her a quizzical look, like she was sorting out a particularly difficult math equation. Finally, she summoned her customer service smile again and told us to sit anywhere we liked. She'd bring us some glasses of water.

We chose a booth by the window, and I slid across the sticky vinyl seats so that I was situated against the glass. A fly worried with a crumb on the windowsill. The Baptist church stood across the street; the towering steeple loomed like a watchtower. Beverly scooted in beside me, and Granny sat opposite us, cigarette already lodged in the rim of the amber glass ashtray. The air was icy, but it smelled of hot grease and bleach water. Marta brought our drinks. Beverly ordered the house salad, Thousand Island dressing on the side. Granny ordered the BLT. I asked for the chicken-fried steak lunch special, double mashed potatoes instead of green beans. My mother would have demanded at least a side of corn, but Granny had other things on her mind than monitoring my vegetable intake.

"Made some good progress this week," she said.

"Did you?" Beverly stirred her ice water absently with a straw. Her sunglasses were nested in her hair. Her eyes and her smile were fixed someplace far away.

"Ten good pages, I think. I'll send what I have with you when you leave so you can help me with some edits and fact-checking."

"Okay."

"Said on the phone you'd have some more research on the UFO angle?"

"What? Oh yes, sorry. You caught me daydreaming."

"Brain still on vacation?"

Beverly had spent last week camping down at Big Bend National Park with her boyfriend, an agriculture major named Hoyle Burnley, who drove a two-tone Bronco and loved nothing more than taking it off-roading into the sweltering heart of the Texas wilderness. Beverly spoke of Hoyle often, and every time she did, jealousy stabbed my heart. I had never met Hoyle, had no reason to dislike him, but I did anyway. I imagined them floating down the Rio Grande in inner tubes, splashing and laughing. Traversing rocky landscapes in that Bronco while a pink-and-orange sunset rushed over the mountains and spilled into the valleys. I could see them together by a campfire, Hoyle's arm around Beverly's shoulder, listening to the wind chase through the sagebrush. I only knew Big Bend from photographs, but my anxious mind formed these images in vivid color.

"Pretty much," said Beverly. "And I have news."

"Well, that's ominous." Granny was smiling, but I could read the worry in her eyes.

"Not bad news."

"Tell it, girl."

"Hoyle asked me to marry him. I told him yes."

Granny reached across the table and took Beverly's hands in hers. They made a stark pair. Beverly had soaked up every ounce of summer sunshine. She appeared relaxed and vibrant and tan. Powerful in her youth, nourished by happiness. Granny's arms were bruised and pale, her hands practically gray. I wished selfishly for some way to transfer just a small bit of that life from one woman to the other.

"Best news I've heard in ages," said Granny. "Long as he's good to you. Don't ever go with any man who treats you poorly."

"He's a good one, Mrs. Edwards."

"Then you have all my best wishes. Both of you."

"I appreciate that. I wasn't sure what you'd think."

"Why would I be anything but happy for you?"

"I know you wouldn't," said Beverly. "But with all that's going on, I don't think I'll have time to work for you in the fall."

"Well, I hate to hear that."

Our food arrived. Granny and Beverly let go of one another to make room. A server named BILLY wearing a hairnet and a white cook's smock placed the dishes before us and withdrew without a word. Beverly started stabbing at her salad with a fork, talking a mile a minute about her class schedule in the fall and the prospect of a winter wedding. Blood pounded in my ears. A wave of heat moved through me, and sweat trailed down my temples. Granny absorbed every word of Beverly's excitement with a pleasant expression, but I could sense her growing smaller as she chewed her BLT and worked to keep any hint of sadness from her eyes. Beverly reminded us that she had her job at the tax office that helped her pay for school, and there was no way she could quit that. And no matter how many times she apologized and promised she'd help Granny find another student to help with research, every word paved a trail toward one inevitable conclusion.

Beverly was leaving us.

There was a better life out there waiting for her.

Tears welled in Granny's eyes, but she assured us they were born of happiness.

"I will miss arguing with you," said Granny.

"I'll still come to visit," said Beverly.

"I'm sure you will."

"And I'm not going anywhere yet. I'll be around until the end of the summer."

"I'll take your help as long as I can get it."

They started talking about the research Beverly had brought along, stuff about supposed alien abductions, lights in the sky, missing time. Nothing I hadn't read about in half the books on Granny's shelves. It all seemed unimportant now. A bone-deep loneliness settled inside me. I couldn't stand the thought of Granny all alone in her haunted house once summer fled.

The town was small, and Granny had lived there long enough for most people to know who she was. But they never welcomed her with anything more than perfunctory greetings and polite queries about her writing. She'd made no real *friends*. No one to look out for her. She was the weird *ghost lady* who moved into the cattle baron's mansion, an outsider in a place where families piled up generations of history, one on top of another. Infiltrating such a close-knit cabal was a task best suited for the young and outgoing, not a terminal middle-aged woman, pining for her dead husband in a creaky old house.

As far as the town was concerned, Granny was already dead and buried.

I read a book once that talked about wolves abandoning dying members of their pack. Casting them out to wander alone. Maybe Granny in her isolation was experiencing something akin to this phenomenon.

Was that the reason I could see the ghosts? Was that the reason other children had no regard for me? Could they sense that my time on earth, like my grandmother's, was quickly winding down?

I slid out of the seat, crawled under the table, and emerged in the booth beside Granny. I leaned in close, put my cheek against her shoulder. Stared across the table at Beverly, our beautiful betrayer. Life lay wide open before her. Her youth afforded every opportunity. Beverly's possibilities advanced while Granny's retreated. And it was the way of things, I understood. But it didn't make the contrast between them any easier to bear.

And though I was only eight, I didn't see those same youthful opportunities in my future.

I felt myself fading.

Chasing death.

Eventually Granny paid the check, and we left the restaurant, every suspicious eye following the ghost lady and her coterie.

Back at the house, Beverly and Granny went to work at the kitchen table, sorting through the boxes of research Beverly brought with her. Shirley wanted to read together, but I was in no mood.

I retreated to my bedroom and haunted the dormer window with Lady Pecan Tree. She ignored me and I ignored her, but together we watched life unfold in the streets of town. One man clutching a ladder, repainting the ornate wooden awning in front of the five-and-dime. Another lazing in the driver's seat of a police car, waiting for a crime that would never occur. Three women with tall hairdos unloaded boxes from the trunk of a brown Buick and carried them through the side door of the church, leaving peals of laughter in their wake. The bicycle gang returned, this time emerging at high speed from between the feedstore and the dress shop, then disappearing around the side of the drugstore. The sun burned golden in the sky, assailed them with its suffocating heat. But the people continued undeterred. They moved and breathed and conducted their mundane affairs, drawing that fire from the sky as fuel for their tiny human endeavors.

None of them spared a glance at our old house.

None of them noticed our longing or our disdain.

And when Beverly finally left, we watched her walk to her car, look up and wave. Lady Pecan Tree remained stoic, but I backed away from the window, robed myself in shadows. The car door slammed. The engine turned over. Wheels whispered down the driveway and into the street. I scurried back to the window, watched Beverly drive away. The sun shone white against her back windshield, and I followed her progress through the streets and onto the highway beyond, uncertain whether I'd ever see her again.

———

Granny spent most mornings furiously typing, like she could feel the flow of time constricting around her and wanted desperately to finish her last book before death came calling. Often, I would sit with my back against the closed door to her den, listening to the *snap snap snap* of keys striking paper. Ghosts would wander through, some friends, some strangers. The floorboards creaked with their passage. The rising sun would sneak in through the stained glass windows and cast rainbows across the wainscotting. Book in hand, I'd wait for her to finish. Every day was another book, but that morning I was reading *Stormbringer*. Again. It was one of my favorites. And I became so absorbed that I didn't hear the typewriter grow silent, didn't notice Granny coming through the door until she opened it wide and sent me crashing at her feet.

"Careful, grace," she said.

"Sorry, I was reading."

She picked up the book where it had fallen out of my hand. Studied the sickly green cover. "*Stormbringer*?"

"Yeah, it's really good."

"Who's this fellow on the cover?"

"That's Elric of Melniboné. And the sword he's holding is Stormbringer. It's got a black blade and was forged by Chaos. And if it cuts you, it drinks your soul."

"And you're old enough to be reading this?"

"You bought it for me. At the news shop."

Granny shrugged, like that was permission enough. She tossed the book back and invited me into the den.

She relaxed into her swivel chair, and I took a seat in the beat-up old recliner that sat in the corner.

"The sword is evil," I said. "Elric doesn't like it much, but he got it from Arioch, who is kind of a demon guy, I guess. It sort of works against Elric sometimes."

"The sword does?"

"Yes ma'am."

"Why doesn't this Eric guy just get rid of the sword?"

"*Elric.*"

"Elric, then. He should just melt it down."

"He can't. He's sick. And the sword gives him power. Without it he's got to take a whole lot of drugs just to stay alive."

"Well, that's a predicament for sure."

Granny appeared more vibrant this morning than usual, rocking a bit in her swivel chair and tapping her feet against the floral tapestry rug. She wore a crimson jumpsuit adorned with silver conchos, and her best wig, chestnut brown with enormous curls. Ever-present turquoise bracelets dangled from her too-slender wrists, moved halfway up her arm every time she raised her hands. Granny was always in pain, but she managed well. And that day she seemed connected to the world in a way that often eluded her.

I loved it when Granny was so energized, but I knew it wouldn't last long. She liked to pretend everything was okay, but I was too smart to believe her.

My parents had argued against my spending the summer with her this year. There was concern I might overwhelm her, as if I was a rambunctious child in need of chasing and tending. Granny and I both threw a fit, and my parents relented. So, when they checked in with their weekly call, no matter what Granny's state, she'd assure them she was the pinnacle of health, and I was the easiest child she'd ever met. Truthfully, she had more bad days than good anymore, but we could both sense the end approaching, and neither of us was ready to abandon our last summer yet.

"I have something I want to give you, Brady."

She spun in her chair, dug into one of her desk drawers, circled back to face me.

She held a necklace: a chunk of smoky brown-and-gray stone, about the size of a silver dollar, attached to a chain. A jagged symbol had been cut into the stone's face, but no matter how hard I tried to focus on it, the lines and the pattern eluded my gaze. Granny held the necklace out to me, stone in one palm, chain draped across the other, like she intended for me to put it on.

"That's for me?" I asked.

"Yes," she said. "Here you go."

"I'm sorry, I don't want it."

Something about the stone compelled me to take it, but I resisted. What would my father think if I came home wearing a necklace? Or the kids at school? That's the sort of *different* that could get a kid beat up.

"What do you mean?"

"I don't want a necklace."

"It's not really a necklace," she said. "Don't think of it that way."

"What is it then?"

"More of a talisman. Like a magic amulet."

"For real?"

"Put it on, and maybe it will grant you powers."

That was enough to overcome my reluctance. I took the amulet, looped it around my neck. The stone sat heavy against my chest. Felt warm through my shirt. Maybe it really held some sort of power. Granny watched intently, like she was expecting a change. I fidgeted with anticipation, but nothing transformed inside me. I was not granted the ability to fly, or the talent to produce fireballs from my palms. But there was something about the amulet, a sort of energy I guess, that calmed me. Perhaps it would reveal its powers in time. But already I was obsessed with it, and I knew I wouldn't take it off, even in the face of terrible scrutiny.

"Thank you," I said.

"You're very welcome," she said. "I want you to keep that close to you. Same as that Elric does his sword."

"But it won't steal my soul?"

"Only a slim chance of that happening."

"What?

"I'm joking, Brady," she said. "Just keep that chain around your neck while you're here, okay? There's a strangeness about this place I don't entirely understand yet. Like everything that's *real* wants to lift up and fly away. Can't have you getting carried off by the wind if that happens. You're already seeing the ghosts. No telling what this place wants from us. Wants from *you*. Seems real easy to lose yourself around here, don't it? Might be some of us are ready to get lost, but you ain't one of them yet, whether you think it or not. So, keep that rock with you. Think of it as a weight, holding you down. Like that chain around your neck binds you to the dirt under your feet."

I gripped the arm of my chair. I understood metaphors, but imagining myself drifting into the sky and losing my hold on the world forever sparked my nerves.

"Do you have a necklace for Beverly?"

"Lord, no. That girl don't need anything to plant her in the material world. She'd do well to visit the clouds now and again. Besides, she won't be coming around much longer."

"Are you sad she's leaving?"

"I surely am. Thought maybe she'd take up and finish the book if...well, if I'm not able to."

Granny let that sentiment linger in the air, like an unpleasant odor.

Eventually, she announced it was lunchtime, left to fix us some ham-and-cheese sandwiches. She didn't ask me to leave her den, so I kept my seat, staring at her towering bookshelves and the messy sprawl of her desk. Whether I'd been granted some new access to her inner sanctum, or she'd simply forgotten to shoo me out of there, I felt emboldened by my circumstances. If Granny couldn't finish her latest book, and Beverly had found more interesting pursuits, then maybe I was the person for the job. I slid out of my seat, climbed up into Granny's swivel chair, and let my fingers rest softly on the typewriter keys. Next to the typewriter sat a stack of pages, and the one she'd been working on that morning lay face up atop the pile.

It read:

We still imagine death as Shakespeare's Undiscovered Country, and yet, we have discovered it, whether we are willing to admit it or not. Death is not an end, but a continuation of our existence, another realm we can access. And like other foreign countries, we can gain entrance to the afterlife if we present the proper credentials. We wander across that border in our dreams. We walk those alien streets during our adventures with entheogens, and we gaze upon those unimaginable skies while in the grip of euphoric religious rituals. And just as we visit that land, its denizens seek passage into ours. Ghosts and fairies. Sea creatures and sasquatch. Little gray aliens. They are not hiding in deep forests or flying here from distant planets. They are close enough to touch, if we are willing to reach out and take their hands.

Perhaps our missing colonists found a place where the border between these two lands is narrow enough to navigate on a material level. Not in their dreams, but in their waking hours. A thin sliver of creation where their bodies could pass from one plane of existence to another. Perhaps they wandered into that Undiscovered County, chasing their dead. And having found all they'd lost, felt no more desire for the land of the living.

Granny had scribbled a few notes here and there in red pen, and she'd circled one bit:

Perhaps they'd wandered into that Undiscovered Country, chasing their dead.

The amulet pulsed against my chest like a second heartbeat.

Granny's *Undiscovered Country* didn't scare me anymore. And if it was like Granny imagined, I couldn't blame those Roanoke people if they went there and never returned.

I wouldn't want to come back either.

———————

Wind battered the house. It passed through the loose places in the walls with a sound like children crying. Storm clouds formed somewhere farther west, began their relentless march, heralded by continuous thunderclaps and blue lightning that cracked the night sky. I lay sweating in bed with a musty old quilt pulled up to my chin, listening to the house being slowly devoured by time. These were the long hours between midnight and daybreak when darkness raged. I wished for Bradbury's lightning-rod salesman to come calling.

Wished I was fearless and fueled with mischief, like Jim Nightshade. Willing to scale the shuddering walls and plant that copper rod on the roof's peak so it might drive the storm away with its strange symbols and esoteric powers.

But no lightning-rod salesman appeared, and I was no Jim Nightshade.

I stayed in bed, afraid to face the stormy night.

Wind caught the house again, gave it a shake. I tried to remind myself this building had stood for a century; no thunderstorm or tornado had claimed it yet. But trapped in the deep heart of night, all my fears and all my nightmares came stalking.

The ghosts were no less agitated. They formed a congress of the dead, barely visible in the shadows, but thrown into stark relief with every lightning strike. Lady Pecan Tree watched the slow approach of the storm, eternal at her window, but the rest of them wandered in circles, drifted across the ceiling, loomed over my bed, watching, like they expected me to do something to quell the violent weather. Shirley lay beside me, on top of the covers, face pressed up against mine, so close I could feel the coldness pouring off her. She never blinked. Never cried. But I could sense her terror. And I wondered, what would happen to them all if the house blew away like the one in *The Wizard of Oz*? Would the ghosts travel with it to some magical land, or would they remain here, homeless, bound to this lonely patch of reality?

I had no clue, and I doubted the ghosts did either.

Somewhere, two stories below my bed, and deeper in the earth, their bones whispered.

"It's okay," I said. "Just a regular storm."

It was true. In the spring, thunderstorms like this were common as copper pennies. Less so this deep in the summer, but not unheard of. Still, I was trying to reassure myself as much as I was Shirley.

"Probably going to rain really hard once it gets here, but I bet it's moving fast. Won't last long."

Glen was pressed against the far wall, boots a few inches off the ground, arms straight down his sides, neck cocked at a sharp angle like he was hanging from a rope. He wore his worried face today, and I was grateful I didn't have to stare at his bare skull every time lightning lit the room. He watched me. They all watched me, save for Lady Pecan Tree. A dozen of them, maybe more. They crowded the shadows, swarming and desperate, and I had that feeling again that they blamed me for the storm, wanted me to make it stop.

I looked for Grandaddy, but he wasn't among them.

I needed him. I was too young to parent all those ghosts myself.

"Have you ever met my grandaddy?" I asked.

Shirley's lips parted, like she was trying to whisper something, but of course she remained silent.

"He's tall as Glen and probably the same age. Mostly I don't remember what he looks like except in pictures. He's been dead a few years. But he didn't die here, so I'm not sure why he lives here now. He worked for the electric company and used to bring me coloring books about Reddy Kilowatt. He liked to carve things out of wood with his pocketknife. Airplanes and arrowheads and stuff. He had a stack of paperback westerns by his chair in the living room and he'd let me play with them, even though I couldn't read yet. I liked the pictures on the covers. Horses and gunfighters and stuff. Have you seen him here? Could you call him, see if he'd come?"

Shirley shifted on the bed. It sounded like sheets of paper rubbing together. But she had nothing to offer about my grandaddy.

"Why won't you ever talk to me?"

Shirley stared at me. Light swimming in her eye.

"Where's Grandaddy? Is he still here?"

Her lips moved again, but she had nothing to say.

"I hate you."

I turned over on my opposite side, so I was facing away from Shirley. I could still feel the weight of her memory against my back.

Being haunted by all these ghosts was becoming a burden. A mystery with no possible solution.

I imagined all the people in town, untroubled by the dead, fast asleep. Unaware of the boy in the drafty old mansion who collected ghosts for friends and lay awake nights, listening for the electric approach of alien spacecraft or the tantalizing call of fairy songs. Was it better to sleep in ignorance or to endure the knowledge that anything imaginable might be real? I don't know. But in that moment, I wished I could banish every terrifying story from my mind, and the ghosts along with them.

All I wanted was to close my eyes and go to sleep.

To be *normal*, for a night.

But the ghosts were unrelenting. They churned in the air like a storm-tossed sea. Restless in a way I'd never seen them. That restlessness infected me. I stood and yanked the quilt from the bed, wrapped it around my shoulders like a cape, and admonished Shirley and the others not to follow. I left the bedroom and proceeded down the groaning wooden staircase in my bare feet and pajamas, quilt trailing behind. My plan was to sleep on the couch, or even the living room floor, with its thick blue rug. Anyplace where the ghosts were not. But at the foot of the stairs, I heard soft music carrying through the night, and saw a sliver of light cut across the downstairs landing like a golden blade.

Instinctively, I grabbed the amulet around my neck. I had named it *Safeheart*. To my ears, an appropriate moniker for a magic stone intended to keep a person grounded and free from harm, yet otherworldly enough I might have plucked it from the pages of a fantasy novel. A name that evoked dangerous quests aided by plucky friends. Because magical artifacts *always* had names. *Safeheart* warmed me. Calmed my nerves. Emboldened me to follow the blade of light back to its source.

Granny was in her den. She'd left the door open just enough so that candlelight spilled out into the darkness.

She hummed along to a song I recognized immediately: "Blue Eyes Crying in the Rain." Willie Nelson was a favorite of hers and a favorite of mine. My Grandaddy had loved him more than either of us did. I approached the door, planning to knock, but something stopped me. The darkness around the door was heavy, and the shaft of light had a shimmery quality that seemed unnatural. *Safeheart* burned against my chest, heavy as a bowling ball. My mouth tasted like pennies, and static lifted the hair on my arms. The music carried on, Willie singing that line about *meeting up yonder someday*, and I got down on my knees, crawled close to the door and peeked into the den, hoping Granny didn't see me. And she didn't. Her eyes were closed. She was in her brown terry cloth bathrobe, seated on the floor with her legs crossed beneath her. Granny had a hard time standing up from her chair by herself some days; I couldn't imagine her maneuvering into such a position. But she had. Wig cast aside so the few tufts of hair on her bald head were visible. Lips mumbling something as she hummed with the music. Trembling, seemingly with exertion, though she was sitting utterly still.

The chairs had been scooted out of the way, the rug rolled back. Granny sat in the center of a circle she'd carved into the floorboards, and various sigils were cut inside the circle, though I couldn't make out most of them. Scattered candles bathed the room in swaying yellow light that drew shadows up the walls and across the bookshelves. The room smelled of sweet incense, and Granny held a chunk of clear quartz the size of a baseball in her hands. Her breaths were long and labored, and I watched closely for the rise and fall of her chest, afraid for a moment she wasn't breathing at all. One song finished; another began. The 8-track console produced a sound that was muddy and rumbling, like one of the speakers had blown, but Willie's voice was still a river of honey, his fingers on the strings quietly beautiful. A long peal of thunder joined the song and shook the walls. Willie sang about being *wild and sorrowful* as tears streaked down Granny's face.

The scene felt intimate, like something I shouldn't be watching. But I lay there with my cheek on the floor, peering through the doorway, wondering what Granny was doing. Her fingers fidgeted with the shimmering quartz. She quit humming, but her lips kept moving. Maybe they formed silent prayers, whispered dark rites, repeated the name of someone she loved over and over again. I don't know. She spoke to the universe, that much I understood. Hard to say whether anyone was listening. But I surely was, and with every word I felt the air grow thicker around me, like I'd fallen in a lake and was struggling to surface.

I crawled away from the door, fearful that if I lingered too long, I wouldn't be able to leave.

The music burrowed through me, and *Safeheart* resonated right along with it. As I crawled down the hallway and into the living room, the amulet seemed to pull me along, to guide me away from whatever was happening in Granny's den. I climbed up onto the couch, pulled my quilt over top of me, and listened to the rain splash against the windows. My heart raced and my ears buzzed. I lay there crying with my face pressed into the upholstery, seized by sadness.

When the room grew suddenly cold, I knew Shirley had followed me. She sat on the floor beside the couch, her chin resting on the seat cushion so that when I turned to face her, our eyes met.

I blinked away tears.

"I don't hate you," I said.

Shirley didn't say anything. She didn't have to. We were *pals.* We understood one another.

For better and for worse.

We often couldn't tell one day from another in that shadow realm of a house, but we judged it was Sunday morning by the plaintive toll of the church bell and the steady flow of finely attired believers past Granny's yard. Polished shoes clapped against the sidewalk, and low voices traded amiable greetings. A few complained about the heat, and others peeled back layers of tinfoil to sneak peeks at the casseroles and Jell-O molds they'd prepared for the fellowship lunch after the service. Some of them waved, and we waved back. But Granny was not a *churchgoer*. So, we remained on the porch with our coffees, Granny with her cigarette, and watched them proceed down the street, marching toward their destination like the upstanding citizens they were.

Granny had been a regular at the Methodist church in her old town, but whatever had drawn her there for so many years had since faded from inside her. It was another thing she argued about with my parents. She liked to say she'd lost her *religion*, but not her *spirituality*. That wasn't something they cared to hear, but no amount of hectoring could reinvest her with the faith she'd lost. My parents insisted on me going, so of course Granny told them she dragged me up the church steps every Sunday. But we spent those mornings on the porch, just like every other day, and kept that secret between us. Church was boring, and the pews were uncomfortable. My mother always clipped a tie too tight at my throat, and shoved my feet into shoes that squished my toes together. I hated going. And so, I counted my absence from worship as another perk of summers spent away from my parents.

Granny hadn't said a word about her activities in the den, and of course I didn't prompt her about it. If the long night taxed her strength, it didn't show. Granny moved slow, like always, but seemed somehow refreshed as she sipped at her morning coffee. In the daylight, with the storm long since moved on, it was easy to imagine the whole thing was a dream, conjured by the ghosts in their fit of pique. Granny talked to me about the progress on her book, and I nodded sagely, as if I was already privy to her plans. A crucial member of the writing team. She expected Beverly to visit again on Tuesday with another box-load of typewritten eyewitness accounts of what she called *high strangeness*, and despite my earlier anger at Beverly, the prospect of her return thrilled me. Perhaps we'd carry on with our endless summer after all, the days unspooling forever in this quietly perfect place.

Then Granny mentioned that my parents would arrive the following weekend to pick me up, and my hopes disappeared.

"I don't want to go home."

"I know, Brady," she said. "Want to know a secret?"

"I guess."

"I don't want to you to go home either."

"Then let me stay."

"Can't. Your parents would miss you. Your friends too. Aren't you excited to start school?"

"No."

"Brady, this is a *sometimes* place, not an *all-the-time* place. I know you don't understand that. But the longer you're around it, the more you start to become a part of it. You don't see ghosts at your house, do you?"

"Sometimes, I think."

"But not most times."

"No ma'am."

"I didn't think so," she said. "Listen, I love you. I want you around as long as possible. But I'm starting to think it was selfish to invite you here this summer. Me in this sorry state. And this place, being what it is. This isn't a bad place, Brady. But that don't mean you're entirely safe here."

"I have a magic amulet." I grasped the stone around my neck and showed her, as if she wasn't the one who'd gifted it to me in the first place.

"Yes, you do, but that don't cure everything."

I knew better than to argue with her. Knew also that it wasn't her fault I had to leave soon. But a knot of resentment settled in my heart, nonetheless.

Granny pushed up from her chair and announced she was going to make us a late breakfast. I stayed by myself on the porch in silent protest, until the clatter of pans and the smell of bacon and eggs drew me back into the house.

The ghosts remained in a state of consternation. Not as frantic as the night before, but inclined to wander and fret about the house, like they were expecting guests and wanted to make sure all preparations were made. When I woke that morning, Shirley had been overhead, clinging to the ceiling like a spider, head wrenched back to keep watch over me. She seemed *thinner* than before. More transparent, even in the comfortable shadows. Something in her eyes gave me the impression she was sick with worry, though whether she worried about me, or about something else, I couldn't say. She followed me around like a puppy, pausing only when I went out on the porch with Granny. But when I came back in, screen door slamming behind, Shirley was there.

My best friend, I guess.

Cold and close as a shadow.

Granny and I ate together at the kitchen table with the pale sunlight pouring in through the windows, and neither of us brought up the sore subject of my imminent departure. Once we finished, she walked to her den, closed the door behind her, started pounding at the typewriter.

I went back into the living room with the tall oak bookcases and let Shirley run her fingers over the spines until she stopped on one that interested her. *A Wizard of Earthsea*. We sat together on the couch, on top of the quilt I'd dragged down from the bedroom the night before, and I read to her the rest of the day. Together we journeyed to that world of wizard schools and dragons and monstrous shadows. And though we'd read it together once before, Shirley hung on every word, appearing every bit as surprised and astonished as the first time. I suppose that is the magic of some books. Shirley sat still as a statue the whole time, but the widening of her eyes and the silent gasp of her mouth signaled her enjoyment. And though she sat so close that the cold caused me to shiver, I pulled the quilt over top of me and continued reading, more content with her than I'd ever been with another person. We read until the sun fell and night flooded in, and I didn't notice my hunger until Granny shook me gently and asked if I wanted anything to eat before it was time for bed.

It was a fine, leisurely day.

I would remember it even more fondly if it hadn't been Granny's last day on earth.

Late that night, Granny tucked me into bed and sat there beside me for a time.

"You awake enough for a story?" she asked.

"Yes, ma'am." I was half asleep already, but I was never one to turn down a story.

"Okay, this one's not really scary."

"It's okay if it is," I said.

"Have I told you about the picture somebody sent me that changes all the time?"

"No, ma'am."

"Well, that's a good story. You'll like it. A woman who lives over in Midland sent me a photograph of her children some years back. Taken out on a farm when they were about your age. It shows the three of them, couple of boys and a little girl, posing real proud for the camera, each one holding a chicken. Nothing real scary about that. But eventually, they noticed other images starting to appear in the picture. A brass clock on a mantel. A tricycle. Just a whole lot of things. And *people* started appearing too. Well, it looked to me like maybe a double exposure, where two pictures sort of mush together. So, we made several copies, sent them to some other folks for their opinion. And things just kept appearing. Same images on every copy of the photo. Same images on all the *negatives*. All of a sudden there's an old-style divan. A man with his arm around a woman, both dressed in clothes from the time when I was a little girl. And that photo never stops changing. Sometimes things fade out, but always things come to replace it. And every copy changes the same. Just this last year I noticed a cat and a dog, faint in the background. Those weren't there before. Called that woman in Midland and sure enough, she spotted them too."

"Are they ghosts in the picture?"

"Ghosts or memories. I don't really know, Brady. Some things we'll never figure out. But we can still enjoy the mystery. Something else. Two of the kids in that picture ended up having close encounters with a horse. The little boy was kicked in the head. The little girl got thrown from a saddle into a barbwire fence. This wasn't long after the picture was taken. Well, neither one of them ended up with so much as a scratch. Which leads me to wonder if the picture protects them somehow. Or maybe the people who appeared there over the years are guardian spirits, loved ones from long ago who are keeping an eye to their safety. This is all speculation, Brady. But it's nice to think maybe folks keep looking out for us, after they're gone."

"Can I see the picture?" I asked.

"Tomorrow, maybe. Right now, it's time for sleep."

Granny leaned over, kissed me on the forehead.

Her lips were colder than her ghosts.

At first, I thought morning had arrived, then I realized it wasn't sunshine pouring in through my upstairs window, but strobing, propulsive blasts of silvery blue light that lit up the room like it was midday. I scrambled out of bed. Lady Pecan Tree stood vigil at the window, and I joined her to see what was outside. Blue light colored the world, so brilliant and bright that I could barely make out the outlines of buildings and street signs and cars parked along the curbs. Dark shapes drifted in the skies, formless and intangible to my eyes. And I could hear people shouting. Screaming. A chorus of children singing. Whatever was happening, my head swam, and I felt queasy. The blue-light pulses caused a steady thrum in the air that burrowed deep into my teeth and my bones. Dizziness set in, and I grabbed the windowsill to steady myself. The world outside shuddered, lurched, began circling around us, like Granny's house was the axis of the universe.

The summer heat was gone, replaced with a blood-deep cold. My panicked breathing fogged the air. I had no idea what was happening, but I understood it must have something to do with Granny's lectures about the unsteady nature of this place.

I hollered for Granny, but all I heard in response was the world-shaking hum that accompanied the light pulses. A painful electrical resonance escaped from the stormy skies and stalking the streets. I placed my hands on the cold window glass, absorbed the vibrations.

Outside, the shimmering shapes in the air began slowly to rise, and I realized with a start they were people, flailing like they were caught in the grip of some invisible god. They were terrified. They were ecstatic. Some of them accepted their fate and ascended with beatific smiles. Others struggled, shouted. Grasped at nothing. I recognized more than one of them. The young preacher from the church. An older couple I'd seen walking their dog through the streets on weekends. Teenagers and toddlers and somebody's mewling baby. The phenomenon, whatever it was, did not discriminate.

People passed through rooftops on their way up. Plucked from their beds, they moved through wood and shingles with no resistance. They grabbed desperately at treetops, but their fingers passed clean through the leaves and branches. They swam in the skies, arms and legs pumping, thinking maybe they could navigate the rising current of gravity and find a way back to shore.

Whatever force compelled them skyward rendered them as immaterial as ghosts.

I ran from my bedroom, hurried downstairs. Maybe if I was closer to earth, there was less chance of me being taken.

The house was alive with ghosts. More than I'd ever seen in one place. They gathered in every room, animated, smiling, almost celebratory. And they had *substance*. Where before they'd been woven of dust and smoke and dreams, now they seemed solid as the furniture. Alive and vital. They absorbed all the blue light pouring in through the windows, mouths moving in silent conversation like people in an old silent film. I struggled to hear them, but I wasn't yet privy to the language of the dead.

Shirley appeared from the crowd with a broad grin on her face that unsettled me, though I couldn't say why. I'd never seen her so happy. She reached out, grabbed my hand. And I could *feel* her fingers entwine with mine. Her skin was warm, and the cold had claimed me entirely. I trembled and shook, freezing in my cotton pajamas and bare feet, lungs still pumping smoke into the crystalline blue air. The room shimmered like glass, and I felt the urge to sit down, go to sleep, and never wake again. Shirley shook me. Rubbed her other hand against my cheek and offered up some of her warmth. I drank it in greedily. I let her pull me close, terrified of what was happening. Shirley had transformed from an idea to something real. And I wasn't sure if she was joining this world, or if I was fading away into another one.

I started crying. Screaming for my grandmother.

Shirley pulled me through the sea of ghosts to the entryway, where the front door stood wide open.

Granny was in the front yard, looking skyward.

I shrieked. Tried to run to her, but Shirley had a tight hold on my arm.

Fierce blue light rained down from a hole in the sky, a wide, quivering opening that *inhaled* people whole. Granny didn't see me. Her arms were raised, and the bottoms of her house shoes were already two feet off the ground. She put up no resistance. The wind growled, and the electrical hum was deep and sonorous. She rose into that terrible blue night with all the others, deafened by an otherworldly wail, blinded by the brilliance of it all. I broke loose from Shirley, leapt at Granny in hopes of grabbing her foot. But she was already too high. She was already gone. She followed all those people who never really understood her into the air and through the veil between our world and another, more eager than the rest to be swallowed up by the mystery.

I leapt into the air again, hoping to be swept up with the rest of them, but gravity prevailed. I hit the ground, stumbled, and fell hard against the sidewalk. That other place didn't want me. I wasn't going *anywhere*. Then I remembered *Safeheart*. I yanked it off my neck, tossed it across the yard. But I was too late. The blue night faded to black again; the stars opened their eyes and gazed down on our empty town.

Granny was gone. *Everyone* was gone.

Except for me and my ghosts.

Beverly Burnley was a ghost come back to life.

She walked into the truck stop diner and I recognized her at once. In her mid-sixties now, but still a striking beauty. I stood and waved her over; she wasn't likely to recognize me after so long. We traded an awkward hug, then she sat across from me in the booth and started fiddling with the saltshaker. Nervous as me, maybe. The waitress slapped menus against the table, and Beverly told me about her grandchildren. I was only half paying attention, struck dumb by the reality of *Beverly Burnley* sitting before me. It was like lunching with bigfoot. A mythical creature escaped from the land of childhood, one you'd always believed existed, but could never prove. That long-ago summer was half a dream now, an alternate universe so very close to this one, yet utterly out of reach. But Beverly was proof it existed. We had explored it together a lifetime ago, and both of us had survived.

"This one's Caden." Beverly scrolled through her phone, tapped the photo on screen with a long, manicured fingernail. "The youngest. He's a little pistol."

"Caden. Good-looking kid. And you have another one, right? A girl."

"Lisa. That's her there." She scrolled again, held up the phone screen so I could see a preteen girl in a blue soccer uniform, ball clutched under one arm.

"She favors you," I said. "Same eyes."

"Yeah, she looks just like I did at that age. Always into something. Caden is a little quieter, though. Likes to read all the time. Reminds me of you at that age."

"Nothing wrong with that," I said. "Long as he knows to come up for air sometimes."

"You allowed to smoke in here?" Beverly put her phone back in her purse, squeezed a lemon wedge into her water.

There was no ashtray, so I'd emptied the saucer full of creamer packets and used that instead. Hadn't even realized I'd lit up. The habit was strong. Something I'd inherited from Granny. Like coffee. Like ghosts.

"Didn't see a sign or anything."

We both knew polite society had moved past smoking sections long ago, but the truck stop was two steps down from a dive, and I doubted anyone would hassle me. When the waitress took our orders without commenting on the smoke, Beverly let it slide too.

Beverly was at least a dozen years older than me, but looked younger by more than a few. She wore an expensive-looking green blouse with tan slacks. Everything about her evinced health and vitality. Her teeth were supernaturally white, her skin was tanned a deep brown. Despite obvious reservations about our meeting, there was a brightness in her eyes, like they'd never gazed on tragedy. And though she hid it well, I knew what she must be thinking. What had the years done to that pudgy little boy with a buzz cut? I fidgeted in my seat, a hulking skeleton, lean and sick and gray. I ran my fingers through what remained of my hair, drew smoke into my lungs, and wondered if she could smell the desperation on me. I'd used the truck stop shower that morning, but there was only so much hardness a person could scrub away.

"I'm happy to see you, Brady," she said. "But why are we here? Other than to catch up, I guess."

"Well, I knew you still lived out this way."

"I don't think you invited me here to talk about my grandkids. Cute as they are."

"I'm going back there," I said. "Wanted to talk to you first. Figured maybe you'd go with me. I don't know."

Something like pity crossed those beautiful eyes, but she hid it in a hurry. "You haven't been back there? Since it happened."

"No, never have."

"Why do you *want* to?"

"What do you think happened, Beverly?"

She took some time to consider my question. Sipped at her water glass with a rigid half-smile on her face. "Ain't That Lonely Yet" played softly from the overhead speakers, and I found myself mouthing the words. When Beverly finally answered, her voice was a whisper, like she was sharing illicit secrets.

"Well, it's a mystery, isn't it. And I don't have a satisfactory answer. I can tell you I don't believe everybody in town was *raptured*. That's ridiculous. But what does that leave? The only reasonable answer is everybody up and left, though I can't say where they went, or for what reason. That's almost as farfetched as the rapture thing. They wouldn't leave everything behind. Their houses and cars. Food in the fridge and bathtubs full of water. They left their *pets*, for God's sake. Nobody does that. But there must be a reasonable explanation, right? I loved your grandmother and her stories, but I don't believe the whole town disappeared into the fairy realm."

"Maybe a UFO took them."

"Now you're just pulling my leg."

"What about Roanoke? You were helping Granny with her book. You read all that stuff about holes in the sky and people disappearing. You don't think that's weird? You two digging up stories like that, and then the same thing happens to her?"

"Sure, it's weird," she said. "And I'll allow it's an amazing coincidence. But people slipping away into another world is fantasy. It's impossible."

"I was there, Beverly. I know what I saw."

"I know you were," she said. "But you were a child. And trauma does strange things to our minds."

"You think I hallucinated it?"

"I don't know, Brady. But I can't believe in a world where people drift away into the clouds and never come back."

I inhaled deep, let the smoke burn in my lungs for a bit. Whether she believed in it or not, that's the world we were living in.

Beverly was the one who found me. *After.* A day or two later, she arrived with her arms full of three-ring binders with a mug of gas station coffee balanced precariously on top. The town was quiet and empty, but she piloted her Datsun through those abandoned streets and up our driveway without noticing the peculiar absence of life. When she pushed open the door with her knee, dusty sunlight flooded in. She called out for my grandmother, then saw me sitting on the floor outside her den. Hands clutching *Safeheart*. Hungry and dirty. Seeing her, I sprang up, wrapped my arms around her waist and started crying. She was like an angel sent to rescue me. *Beverly would understand.* I told her everything that happened. She called out for Granny again. Eventually searched the house and realized she was gone. Beverly told me to follow, and we walked down to the town square. Knocked on doors, peered into the windows at the café. Yelled out for signs of life. The longer we kept this up without answer, the more terrified Beverly became. *Everybody* was gone. Eventually she put me in the passenger's seat of her car and drove us back to her house. She peppered me with questions for forty miles, but I'd already told her everything I knew. When my parents came to get me, they asked all those same questions all over again. None of my answers were satisfactory, and nobody wanted to hear the one thing of which I was certain.

Granny had been chasing after *something*.

And I was pretty sure she'd found it.

"I wasn't making anything up," I said. "I remember exactly what happened."

The waitress delivered our food. I snubbed out my cigarette. Unrolled my napkin and let the silverware clatter against the tabletop. The burger I'd ordered looked half burned, but I wasn't picky. Beverly lifted the top slice of bread off her BLT and slathered it in mayonnaise.

"I know what you told me then," she said. "But you're an adult now. What's your explanation for it?"

"Well, I've had plenty of time to think on that."

"And what have you determined?"

"Granny really opened a portal. She found a hole in reality that people can pass through, from one dimension to another."

"Brady…"

"I used to see ghosts in that house," I said.

Beverly seemed unsure how to respond to that. When finally she spoke, it was with false enthusiasm, like she was throwing me a lifeline. "My mother saw a ghost once. Floating alongside the highway like some hitchhiker. Disappeared when she got close. I'd have told that story to your grandmother, but this was after."

"There were a *lot* of ghosts in that house," I said. "It was a strange place."

"Was your grandmother able to see them too?"

I nodded. "Yeah, sometimes."

"But nobody else could see them? Just you and her."

I pushed my plate to the side, just a single bite taken from my burger. Eating was hard. Most times, food made me nauseous. Pain swelled in my chest and in my stomach, and I downed my half glass of water, eager for a refill.

"Some of us are closer to death than others," I said.

"Okay?"

"I mean, even when we're kids. Some people live their whole lives so close to death they can smell the grave. Makes them open to places where the line between life and death is skinny, like that house. You can see the ghosts leaking through from some other place."

"Like another world, then?"

"Yeah, I think *death* is just another dimension of reality. Does that make sense? Like you can cross back and forth. That's my theory at least."

"So, if all that's true, why do you want to go back?"

"You called it a mystery, right? I want to solve it."

"You sure there's not more to it than that?"

Beverly delivered this friendly challenge with a mischievous grin, and it rekindled my memories of her good-natured arguments with Granny.

I was grateful Beverly had agreed to meet me. Grateful she was at least *listening*. When I'd tracked her down on Facebook, there was no reason for her to feel obliged to talk, but she'd friended me at once and we'd messaged for a few months before my invitation to meet for lunch. Now she sat here, prim and pleasant and smelling of lavender, entertaining my wild theories. Taking delicate bites of her sandwich while her eyes studied my harried state of being, and forgave it.

"All the people who vanished," I said. "I think I can help them. Give them a chance to come back."

"They've been gone a long time, Brady."

"Maybe time works different there."

"*Maybe* isn't a commodity you can trade in for long, less you want to go broke."

"I know all of this is crazy. But I believe it. Whatever that says about me. And I've got to at least try, while I still can. All those people are gone because of Granny. Not that she intended any of that to happen."

"You're saying she caused it."

"Granny just wanted to find Grandaddy."

"He died a few years before that, right?"

"Yes, but he was there. On the other side of the line between our world and that otherworld. She spent every day trying to get to him, and once she did...well, I guess she took a lot of people with her on accident."

Beverly ate quietly while we spoke. No doubt sure I was crazy, but too nice to say so.

"You don't have to believe me," I said. "I just appreciate you hearing me out."

"I don't want to sound unkind," she said. "But what's my part in all this?"

Part of me hoped Beverly might have some extra clue, some memory of Granny's mindset that summer, but most of me knew better. Beverly was happy; her life was sorted. A quick scan of her social media showed a smiling family on beach vacations and holidays in snowy mountain cabins. That long-ago summer didn't own her like it did me. But she was still the only person who might understand what drove me to go back there.

"I just wanted to see you, Beverly. That summer turned my life a different direction, literally, and you're the only touchstone I have from that time."

"I don't know what I can do to help."

"You don't have to. Really."

"I just...if I could do something I would."

"Like I said, I'm going back. Today."

"Wait, today?" she said.

"Soon as we finish eating," I said. "The town is what, thirty miles from here?"

"Give or take."

"My plan is to spend the summer there. See what I can figure out. Maybe you want to drive out there with me?"

"The town's abandoned, Brady," she said. "It's not even a tourist trap anymore."

"I know that. I'm prepared."

"I mean, there's no water. There's no electricity."

"I know that too."

Something shifted in the way Beverly regarded me. Like she'd finally sorted out I wasn't sweet little Brady with his nose in a book anymore. I was a fifty-something man with a broken soul, who might be crazy, and maybe a little dangerous. I don't think she was right about me. But it's hard to say. What scraps of life I'd managed to pull together over the years had all been blown away. And I'd let them drift off into the wind with no effort to catch them. Fading away was so much easier.

Nothing bound me to this world anymore.

"I'll follow you out there." Beverly caught herself staring, summoned her smile again. "Make sure you're okay? But I can't stay long."

"Thank you," I said. "Means a lot. And I don't expect you to stay. Just need someone to know where I am, I guess. If that makes sense."

The waitress left the check, and Beverly insisted on paying. Scribbled down a tip and shoved her wallet back into her purse. When we left, I opened the door, invited her out into the heat of the day. She smiled, said thanks, but she'd developed a deep melancholy.

"You really saw ghosts in that house?" she said.

"Yeah, I really did."

"I never did. I've never seen one anywhere."

"Well, maybe today's the day."

———

We drove separately, Beverly tailing me in her Lincoln Navigator, every mile marker bringing us closer to the place where everything had gone sideways.

Weathered billboards along the interstate encouraged people to visit *Rapture Town, The Holiest Little Town in all of West Texas*, though whatever interest the public once had in the place had faded along with the colors on the signs. Some megachurch out of Dallas had bought the whole town in the mid-eighties, turned it into a destination where *families could gaze skyward into the waiting arms of God!* Supposedly there had been vendors selling food and trinkets, and recreations of the blessed event using wires and harnesses to whisk true believers into the brilliant blue skies. A playground was established for children in the vacant lot across from the old Baptist church, and tours of that stoic building related the life story of the preacher who'd presided on that blessed day, a man everyone in town had called Preacher Mike, but if the billboards were to be believed, was forever after known as Saint Mike.

Rapture Town was a regular boomtown all through the nineties, until evidently the donations slowed, and the holy site was ceded to the rattlesnakes and the horny toads.

And the ghosts, I guess.

West Texas was still a cauldron of wind and dirt, and I could feel it buffeting my old white Malibu as I left the interstate and navigated the short drive to town.

Upon arriving, we found every street blocked by concrete barriers, but an expansive caliche parking lot had been built to accommodate all the church busses, so I parked there, and Beverly pulled in beside me. She wore designer sunglasses, and a scarf to shield her hair from the wind. Beverly looked more out of place here than ever. She regarded my car with undisguised alarm. Everything I owned was squeezed tightly into the back seat: faded tee shirts and torn jeans, yellowed paperback books and CDs, a few stained pots and pans. Sheets and blankets wadded into a ball, and my old Sears guitar with two of the strings snapped.

Ephemera of a grim life not well lived.

Evidence of someone leaving their apartment in a hurry, with no plans on going back and no safe destination in mind.

"Are you doing all right?" Beverly asked.

What she'd wanted to ask was, *Are you living in your car*, but the obvious answer made her uncomfortable.

"Doing great now that we're here. Let's look around."

Before she could summon more questions about my well-being, I marched through the tall weeds and made my way into *Rapture Town*.

Before, Granny's house had been uniquely unsettling; now the whole town was full of haunted houses, every one of them leaning and broken, like headstones in a long-abandoned cemetery. Graffiti decorated the walls of the buildings on the town square, and every plate glass window was cracked or shattered or missing altogether. Tumbleweeds hugged up against the foundations and clogged the alleyways, and islands of sand shifted through the streets like great crawling snakes, touched by the wind and startled into motion. The playground equipment was all rusted, every swing seat missing from its chain, and all the *Rapture Town* food stands and knickknack booths had fallen in on themselves, reduced to stacks of kindling awaiting a bonfire. A tall chain-link fence topped with razor wire surrounded the church, evidently intended to preserve at least one holy site amid the departure of commerce, but bullet holes marred the high stained glass windows, and knots of weedy brush and mesquite trees crowded the perimeter of the building on all sides.

"It's like Sleeping Beauty." Beverly laced her fingers through the chain link, gave it a rattle, like she might be able to pull it down.

"It's what?" I asked.

"Like a castle surrounded by brambles? With a princess inside. Sleeping Beauty."

"Oh yeah, sure."

We walked past the café, peered in through a broken window and saw evidence of animals living inside. Weeds grew a foot high through the cracks in the sidewalk, and bricks had fallen off the front of the building and toppled into the street. I wasn't sure if that church in Dallas still owned the land, or if everything had been sold to someone else, but it was evident no one had visited in a very long time. The town felt like it was waiting for salvation. A spark of life to reignite old memories.

"This is a real live ghost town," said Beverly.

"Funny," I said.

"I don't know what I was expecting," she said. "But it was something different than this. I mean, it's kind of sad, right? Like there's nothing left here worth resurrecting. Better to let nature have it."

The town didn't feel that way to me at all, but I didn't want to argue.

Rapture Town was dead, but I was pretty sure I could bring it back to life again.

We rounded the edge of the drugstore building, and could see Granny's house a couple of blocks up the street. My heart raced with four decades of fear and anticipation.

Part of me expected Granny's house to be gone, to *never have existed*. Like maybe my memories of that summer were cobbled together from storybooks and an unreliable imagination. But it still stood strong. Years of blowing sand had stripped away much of the color from the siding and the wooden shutters, and the windows were filthy and scratched, leaving only a murky impression of what lay inside. But there was no graffiti on the house, no bullet holes or broken glass. Even the stained glass front door with its colorful cattle drive remained surprisingly unmolested.

We drew closer. Reached the picket fence surrounding the front yard. But I couldn't pass through the gate yet. I grabbed the fence posts with both hands, breathed deep, let my eyes follow the rise of the house until they found the dormer window in my old bedroom. The one with the view of the whole town and miles of farmland beyond. The window that Lady Pecan Tree claimed as her own. And though the windows were muddied, and the reflected sunlight was enough to blind a person, I saw her there. Barely formed and thin as smoke, but Lady Pecan Tree remained in her spot.

I went down on my knees, buried my face in my hands, and started to cry.

"Brady, are you okay?" Beverly knelt beside me, put a hand on my shoulder. "What's happening?"

"She's here," I said. "This is all real."

"Please stand up," said Beverly. "You're scaring me."

I didn't stand, but I looked up and saw ghosts haunting other windows. New faces and old. Including Shirley, who peered out from the living room window, tiny hands against the glass, fading in and out of focus.

The ghosts were all still here. *Waiting.*

"Everything is fine," I said. "Just didn't realize how overwhelmed I'd be coming here."

"I'm sure it's hard." Beverly fretted, kept trying to pull me up, like coaxing me into a standing position would put the world right again. Eventually I relented.

Stood and brushed the dirt off my pants. Beverly eyed the house with worry, but it was for my sake. She couldn't see the ghosts.

She'd *never* see the ghosts.

"You're nice to come out here with me," I said. "I know all this seems crazy."

"I don't think that."

"You do," I said. "But it's okay."

"You can't really mean to stay here," she said.

"My trunk is full of canned food, water. Bunch of other stuff. I'll be fine for a while."

"I can't leave you here by yourself."

"Yes, you can."

Beverly appeared fraught. Trapped between memories of little boy Brady and the thoroughly troubled adult standing before her. Her intentions were in the right place, but I was still a stranger with dangerous motives.

"Told Hoyle I'd be home by three…"

"Please, I promise it's okay. Go ahead. You know where to find me if anything happens."

It took me another ten minutes to convince Beverly to leave. As much as I'd desperately wanted her to come with me, to look upon this place and see how her memories compared with mine, now I wanted to be alone.

Standing in Granny's yard, with every ghost watching, I felt like this was the home I'd been searching for my whole life.

———

In the wake of the disappearances, once it was evident that none of those who left would be returning, my parents held an estate sale, allowed people to rummage through Granny's belongings and fill their pickup truck beds with all her memories. Others with family missing had done the same. Unsure how to politely dispose of so many vacated lives, they carried on in this practical fashion. Whatever wasn't picked over was left behind, and so Granny's house wasn't bare, but still populated with many of my favorite things. All the furniture in the living room was gone, as were all the appliances. But the kitchen table where Beverly and Granny liked to pore over their papers was still there. So were the flowered curtains and the musty rugs and the old steamer trunk she kept in the hallway to store throw blankets and extra linens.

The heat when I entered the house was stifling, but the place was far cleaner than I expected. No covering of sand atop every surface. No animal smell to indicate some creature made its den here. Other than half of everything missing, the house was as it had been.

I imagined ghosts flitting about the hallways, sweeping the floors. Polishing the furniture. An impossible notion that nevertheless conjured a smile.

The ghosts were content to watch my progress from the shadows, so far unwilling to engage.

The floorboards creaked the same tune as always when I made my way down the hall. I opened the door to Granny's den. And it was all still there, or most of it. Her desk. Her sturdy black typewriter. Every curious book and every half-melted candle. Nothing had been disturbed. Why hadn't anyone raided this room during the estate sale? It seemed impossible. The room gave off the eerie sensation that it had been waiting for me. I was no longer a child with restricted access, but a desperate adult with the will to divine all its secrets.

The rug was rolled away, and Granny's magic circle was still visible on the floor. I knelt, ran my fingers along the carved path of the symbols she'd left behind.

All of it made so much more sense to me now.

I started coughing. Every dry hack felt like a fishhook in my lung. Blood spattered the floor, and I wiped the residue off my lips with my shirtsleeve.

The day had required more of my body than I could give. I lay there on the floor, safe in Granny's circle. Figured it was as good a place as any other to sleep.

Sometime in the early evening, music began to play. Willie Nelson. "Sad Songs and Waltzes." Maybe it was in my head, or maybe it spilled softly from Granny's old 8-track player that was still on the shelf. No matter. Nothing could place me back in childhood like the sound of Willie's voice. I might have been eight years old again, lying there crying and wishing I wasn't so alone. I thought about all the songs Granny never got to hear. The ones recorded after that she would have loved. "Always on My Mind." "City of New Orleans." "Your Memory Won't Die in My Grave." Death was coming, and I was ready. But I couldn't help but think about all tomorrow's songs I'd never hear. The music washed over me as I drifted in and out of consciousness, and I wondered at the way his voice could bridge yesterday and today.

When I was dead, music would be the only thing worth missing.

But if we can carry anything with us to the afterlife, I had to believe it was music.

Sometime deep in the night, Shirley joined me.

She sat on the floor, her eyes shut tight, listening.

When night finally faded, the music left with it.

———————

Months ago, I'd resolved to die in that house, or to find my way to that other realm first.

Time was short either way.

My cancer was a different sort than Granny's, but no less final. Treatment was over, and there was nothing left to bind me to the world. I'd sold everything that wouldn't fit in my car, left my tiny Dallas apartment mid-lease.

Whatever happened next, I wouldn't be leaving.

What I'd told Beverly about rescuing the souls who'd gone missing was true; my hope was that in opening the portal again, my revised version of Granny's spell would call them all home again. If Granny was right, most of them wouldn't want to return, but they at least deserved the chance. While they were coming, though, I'd be going. Assuming everything worked out like I hoped. I'd read through all the books Granny had written so many times the covers had fallen off. And I read *between the lines*. She was writing about ghosts and cryptids and aliens, sure. But she was also writing about how those things belonged in the everyday world, and only our perceptions of reality made them anything other than organic parts of our existence. Throw in all the books I recalled seeing on her shelf, and all the ones I'd heard her mention, and Granny had laid out a road map to reach beyond the material world and into the mystery.

All I had to do was follow.

After a lifetime of study, I considered myself no less of an occult expert than Granny had been. Which meant nothing in the grand scheme of things.

Mistakes were still easy to make.

The first week in the house, I became reacquainted with the ghosts. Everything in my car I moved into the living room, and Shirley eyed all my books with envy, choosing one every day like she used to. We read aloud, and she listened raptly to my pained, papery voice. During the bright hot days, we read *The Last Unicorn* and *Prince Caspian*. But when night fell, we'd plant a sputtering candle between us and read short stories by Kelly Link and Mary Rickert, writers I knew Shirley would love. Even Glen the cowboy would join us sometimes, drawn in by the candlelight, leaning up against the wall with his boots barely touching the floor. When the story was particularly good, others would crowd in, smoky and writhing and dim in the darkness. It was as if time stood still. Like the stories of their afterlives had paused, and restarted again with my return. How had they spent their time in my absence? Had they even realized I was gone? Pity consumed me for a time, then I realized we shared the same sort of stagnancy. My life hadn't amounted to much, and now I was back in that old, haunted house, commiserating with the dead.

This was my resting place too, and nobody was going to come looking for me.

Being the only person left behind in a town full of the *raptured* had confirmed every fear my parents had about me, and though I was only a child, they gave up on my soul without much of a fight.

God didn't want me, so why should they?

We hadn't spoken in years, and every friend I'd made vanished long ago. There had been a lonely job as a night watchman, a few coworkers I'd chat with during shift changes, but those were gone too. Beverly was the only living soul who knew where I was, and she was practically a stranger.

It felt so odd not to be *known* by anyone.

My second week back, we dug through everything in Granny's den, Shirley guiding me to each nook and cranny where Granny had stashed cassette tapes, unpublished manuscripts, and all her treasured photographs. The fact that my parents had left that stuff behind always caused tension between us, and I'd assumed every memory of Granny's research had been swallowed up by time. Finding it all there waiting for me was overwhelming, and I sat for long hours at the desk, fingers running over the surface of the photos she'd shown me in my youth and all the ones she'd judged too terrifying to reveal at the time.

One of them showed a screaming toddler levitating upside down inside a dilapidated barn, yellow pigtails dangling. A white-haired old man in overalls reached up his hands, tried to keep her from floating away, his face slack with wonder. Another photo showed a dead woman in an ankle-length dress, lying face up on a brass bed. Blood soaked the bed quilt beneath her and stained the wall behind the headboard. A smoky blue cloud covered the shape of the woman, like she was wearing her own ghost, and the face it wore was locked in a horrified scream.

There were hundreds of these. Maybe thousands.

"Granny was right," I said. "Probably best she didn't show me some of these."

Shirley didn't comment, but she stood beside my chair, eyes on the sprawling mess of photos like she was making an intense study of them. I recalled the night Granny opened the portal, the way Shirley had been able to grab ahold and drag me along with her. At the time I believed she'd become temporarily *physical*, but after years of consideration, I wondered if it wasn't the other way around. Like I'd grown thin and spectral, a ghost of myself. And in such a state, Shirley and I had become the same sort of half-alive creature.

It was a part of the mystery I still hadn't solved.

Shirley pointed to a particular photograph, and I dug it out from the pile. No ghosts this time. Just Granny and me, posing on the front porch, both of us grinning and wet with summer sweat. Must have been Beverly who took it, and it must have been close to the end. Granny was nothing but bones.

While I'd known how sick she was, I never reckoned the sort of pain she endured. Living with it myself now, it made me wish I'd done more to help her.

I slid out of the chair and moved gingerly to the ground. Arranged myself cross-legged in the center of Granny's magic circle.

Shirley watched from the edge of the circle.

For an hour or so, I chanted. Called on forces outside the material world to grant me access to the mystery. Worked my magic the very way Granny had, though hopefully in such a manner that I'd be able to better control the outcome. For a long time, I'd tried to find that one spell she must have used to open the portal. But eventually I realized it was an ongoing process, a protracted prayer to the universe that required not only the right words and intentions, but the right environmental conditions. All my spell work. All my time communing with ghosts. Every day spent dying here in this house served to *loosen the environment* so that when the time was right, that other world would open its eye and see me waiting.

Every day my sickness drew me closer to death.

And death drew me closer to the mystery.

By the time I finished my chants, the shadows had grown long. Candlelight colored the room, though I hadn't moved from the circle. Maybe Shirley lit the candles. Maybe the house held more secrets than I'd imagined.

None of that mattered anymore.

Summer was here, and all of this would soon be over.

————————

Granny's Adirondack chair still occupied the same spot on the front porch, and I'd spend mornings seated there, sipping black coffee made on my propane camp stove. In the evenings, I'd smoke an endless procession of Marlboro Reds, leaving my ash in the same Maxwell House coffee can Granny had used. I couldn't recall either the chair or the can being present when I'd first returned to the house, but eventually they revealed themselves to me, undisturbed by time, like they'd been carefully packed away and stored for my eventual return. No light remained in town to wipe away the stars, so they capered across the skies like flocks of jeweled birds, and I'd watch them spin and dive and chase one another across the universe.

One morning as I lazed on the porch, I saw someone trekking up the street from the center of town. The sun was barely up, and it had rained the night before. The heat of the day hadn't yet chased away the dew. I'd forgotten the way West Texas rain always smelled *dusty*, and as I watched the person approach, I breathed the morning deep into my lungs. At first, I assumed this was a waking dream, a ghost, or a memory of someone I remembered from town. Every day back in the house taught me how malleable reality had become in this place. But when the figure drew closer, I recognized Beverly, carrying two paper sacks filled with groceries.

She came onto the porch, put the sacks down, and sat in the chair opposite mine. "So, you're still here then."

"All settled in," I said. "You didn't have to bring anything."

"You need to eat, right?" she said. "Unless the grocery store is back in business."

"I brought a lot of food with me. Canned veggies. Chips and stuff."

"Well, now you have some fresh fruit. Some bread."

"Beverly, you don't really even know me."

"Listen, I sort of felt bad for leaving you here. Your choice to stay, I know. But you seem like you could use some help. Sorry if I'm offering up pity you don't want, but I'm just telling you how I see it. I think you're crazy for staying here, but you seem determined."

Truth be told, even if it was pity that brought here there, I was glad to see her. As much as I loved the ghosts, their company wasn't entirely fulfilling. Just hearing another person speaking aloud proved a tonic for my loneliness. The ghosts never ventured onto the porch, but I could feel them pressing up against the walls. Listening. Maybe curious about what happened beyond the borders of their insulated existence.

"I appreciate the food," I said. "And the visit."

"And the house is safe to live in?"

"Sure. Want to take a look inside?"

"No, I'd rather talk out here on the porch, if you don't mind."

And so, we did. We talked about Granny and the work Beverly did for her. We talked about Beverly's life with Hoyle, and about the joyful raising of their children. She related her memories of me from that summer, and we laughed about the way I was too shy to speak much around her. She asked about my life, and I revealed the truth. My fraught childhood in the wake of the disappearances. My unfulfilled friendships and fleeting human connections. The fact that I was too absorbed in what happened to Granny, what happened to *me*, to invest any real effort into a normal existence. Beverly listened with a grim expression when I explained the severity of my diagnosis, and when I detailed the painful path that led me back to the town where I should have died.

We talked for hours. And when Beverly left, she promised to return.

In this way, we fell into our old routine. Beverly visited the house every week or so, her armloads of research material now replaced with bottled water, butter cookies, and cans of Campbell's chicken noodle soup.

After that first visit, we conducted our conversations indoors, and she commented on the surprising tidiness of the place, despite long abandonment. I could neither explain nor take credit, so I smiled and mumbled something about Granny always keeping a clean house, and she'd want it that way. Like always, Beverly's vitality drove every ghost to the shadows, but they listened intently to our conversations, and I believe they appreciated the visits as much as I did. Beverly still couldn't see them, but I described each of them in detail, and shared my imagined stories about their lives. I'm not sure if Beverly believed, but she listened. And that was more than most would have done.

One scorching-hot afternoon in the deep middle of summer, we sat at the kitchen table playing hand after hand of gin, and while I was shuffling the cards, Beverly leaned back in her chair and revealed her philosophy about death.

"I believe in the human soul," she said. "I just can't say for sure where it goes when we die."

"Don't worry," I said. "Poets and songwriters don't know either, and they've been trying to figure it out since forever."

"I don't think we end up angels on clouds with golden harps," she said. "But I also don't think we burn in a pit of fire because we stole a tube of lipstick from the Woolworth's when we were eleven."

"You're a makeup thief, huh?" I dealt the cards, loving the whispery sound they made as they traversed the tabletop. I recalled Grandaddy teaching me to play gin at a rickety old card table when I was far too young to really understand the game. Granny helping me perfect it during our summers together. We'd always engage in good-natured trash-talking, and more often than not I'd come up on the losing end. But who won never mattered. Card games and dominoes occupied many of my happiest memories of childhood.

"Yeah, once upon a time," she said.

"I'll keep a close watch on my eyeliner."

"There's *something* after we die," she said. "I know that in my bones. I can't believe in an eternity of just...I don't know. I hope we get to choose what happens to us, or maybe we can do all kinds of things."

"What do you mean?"

"Lot of cultures believe you have more than one soul. Like the yin and yang in China? One soul for the afterlife, and one stays behind. I think that's right? Maybe we have a lot of different parts to our soul, and they all go on their own adventures. That sounds a lot more fun than spending eternity in one place, right?"

"Does to me." I arranged the cards in my hand, knowing already it was a mess, and I was likely to lose this round. Shirley braved an approach. Sat in one of the empty chairs with her chin rested on the tabletop. She eyed Beverly warily, my endorsement of her character not quite enough to banish Shirley's concerns about the living.

Beverly's practical leanings still existed, and any time our conversations tended toward the metaphysical, she dusted off her science. But her notion of multipart souls reminded me of her affinity for cultural exploration, for folktales and strangeness. Having all of that in her heart is what convinced Granny to hire her as an assistant in the first place. Her personality diverged in contradictory ways, and that itself seemed evidence enough that Beverly might be right about bits of our souls winding up different places after our deaths. Maybe each part of us wanted something different.

It was a notion I'd examined from every angle over the years, and one that made a great deal of sense. And I'd come to wonder if death was even a requirement for splitting the soul. Some part of me had surely remained behind, in this place, when I left it those many years ago. For a long time, I thought of the house as having captured me. Like part of my being was its eternal prisoner. But as the years progressed, I began to think it was the other way around. I'd taken the house and its mysteries inside me, locked it up tight in my heart. Always close, but inaccessible. Maybe that spark of young Brady I'd left behind was the only key that could unlock the cage, set it free. Maybe I'd left part of myself there for that reason.

I discarded a seven of diamonds, and Beverly snatched it up right away.

"None of that means I believe in ghosts," she said.

"Sounds like you do to me."

"I don't *not* believe in ghosts either," she said.

"Well, that's a start," I said.

Shirley leaned over, and I showed her my hand. Maybe she understood the rules, or maybe she was just bored. Either way, she nodded like my victory was assured.

I drew another card, wondered if this was the only *instance* of Shirley, or if other pieces of her soul wandered strange dimensions, knee-deep in exhilarating adventures. Wondered if pieces of myself had already broken off to chase her through those mythical fields. It wouldn't surprise me. I'd always felt half a person, and the closer I came to death, the more every part of my soul filled with wonder. There was no fear. No real trepidation. Just an all-consuming desire to *understand*. Given infinite afterlives, I'd explore all the perilous fantasy lands I'd read about, wield every sentient sword, cast every chaotic spell. I'd play endless hands of forty-two and spades and gin with the people I loved, and all the friends I'd never made. I'd bike around the neighborhood causing trouble, and explore the galaxy from the bridge of my own space cruiser. No corner of reality would remain uncharted. No hidden treasures would go undiscovered.

And I'd spend forever in my haunted house, the only place I ever lived where I wasn't entirely alone.

The only place I ever felt safe.

"Might see something around here that changes your mind," I said. "There's plenty to see."

"Maybe I will. I love telling stories, imagining fantastical things. But I need something concrete before I believe any of it. You know, I hope you're right. Don't think I wouldn't rather live in a world of ghosts and sprites. Bigfoot hitching a ride with aliens. A portal to Narnia."

"Technically, I don't think Narnia exists."

"Still, it would be cool."

"The universe has to keep some of its secrets."

"You see ghosts though," she said. "Or you think you do, no offense."

"Sure."

"That's the universe revealing *something* then."

"Yeah, but death is the secret the universe holds closest to its heart. If we knew for sure what happens when we die, I figure all the preachers would be out of business in a hurry."

"I'm in no rush to die," she said. "But I can't wait to find out."

"Tell you what," I said. "I'll know soon enough. If you want, I'll come back and give you all the spoilers."

My joke fell flat, and fear swam in Beverly's eyes. Imagining how one day soon, she might show up with her bags of saltine crackers and canned sodas, and find me dead on the kitchen floor. Our time here together was fleeting, supernatural arguments aside. Whether the portal swallowed me, or death took me first, the clock was quickly winding down. Sadness settled inside my heart again, and I realized I was mourning the loss of Beverly, like she was the one dying. Mourning the loss of Shirley too, and all the other ghosts who'd come together and given me the sort of mindful peace I hadn't felt in a very long time. And though I firmly wished for death, leaving these friends behind would be a hardship I hadn't counted on.

"You don't need to be in a hurry either," she said.

"Don't worry. We've got a few hands left yet."

"Speaking of," she said.

"Yeah?"

Beverly splayed her winning cards across the table. "Gin."

———

Every night, when the summer sun fell beyond the horizon, the house came to life. Candlelight spilled down the walls like golden honey, and mesquite logs blazed in the brick fireplace, causing the whole house to become impossibly cold, like the flames themselves captured the summer heat and held it at bay. I would throw on a sweatshirt, wrap a quilt around my shoulders, and lounge on the living room sofa that had somehow returned from the void. Music drifted in the night like a ship on quiet seas. It was Willie Nelson, *always*. But I never tired of that voice. I don't know if the ghosts were responsible for these tiny miracles, or if some other power drove these things into existence, but I wallowed in the uncanny beauty of it just the same.

Ghosts crowded every inch of the house in the deep middle of the night. Not just the residents I'd grown close to, but strangers. Travelers from unknowable places. They gave off that mothy, bookish smell and stirred up clouds of dust as they drifted from room to room, engaged in quiet conversations that eluded my understanding. Garbed in derby hats and buffalo robes and tall black boots. Calico dresses, spring bonnets, and long flowing capes. They were time travelers, returned from long ago. Shirley and the other denizens of the house welcomed these newcomers to their afterlife soiree as honored guests. They mingled together in a shimmery sort of dance; their movements sounded like someone sweeping the floorboards. For the most part, they ignored me, but occasionally one of them would cast an expectant glance in my direction, as if gauging how close I was to joining them in death. I would acknowledge them with a nod, all the while feeling myself growing less and less substantial. A living skeleton. Close to death, but not yet close enough for the party.

Pain ravaged my insides, and my breathing came in slow bursts. Some days were better than others, but in the nighttime, the pain was always ferocious.

Despite this, I devoted time every night to the magic circle, stoking my ongoing ritual, but matters seemed to be progressing with or without my input. The way the house breathed and moved and issued invitations to the dead was evidence of that. Granny's ball of quartz felt fiery hot in my hands, and her words felt right on my lips. Every angle and action had been pursued, and I had no doubt the portal would open wide and swallow me before the arrival of autumn. Assuming I lived so long. The ghosts mostly left me alone in the circle now. They had their own business to attend to in the deep night. But when I finished my rituals, the living room couch was always waiting, and the party was always festive.

One night the pain became so immense, I couldn't rise from the couch and climb the stairs to my bed. So, I dozed in and out of sleep there in the living room, surrounded by ghosts, drunk on their shimmery beauty. I lay with a pillow propped under my head, beneath a quilt that Granny's mother had made, watching the ghosts drift in and out of the room. I watched closely, wondering if I might recognize any of the town's vanished souls. But I never did. Those people were gone. They'd left no ghosts behind. And I think that's because none of them were meant to go.

None of them were *dead*.

I'd begun to realize that despite my good intentions, calling them all home again was likely folly. I could lay a path for them, but I could never make them follow it.

If that other world was anything like I envisioned, it was hard to imagine any of them wanting to come back.

Shirley came to check on me. Placed her hand against my forehead, and I could feel the coolness of it.

She wore a worried face.

I wanted so very much to die, to leave forever.

Shirley turned my head with her cold hands, and I gazed through the crowd and saw Granny, standing outside the living room door, near the foot of the stairs. My heart caught in my throat. She wore brown polyester slacks and a green turtleneck sweater. Her auburn hair had grown back and was coifed high on her head, like she'd just come back from the beauty parlor. Turquoise and onyx and jade adorned her wrists, and her face was flush with color. Granny had found her vitality in death. No longer a skeleton, no longer stooped and grim. Granny appeared as transparent as a memory, but it was her. I tried to sit up in a hurry, screamed in pain. Granny waited patiently as Shirley helped me into a seated position, and then to my feet. I was afraid of what it might mean, that I could feel Shirley's insistent touch. I shuffled across the rug, asking ghosts for forgiveness as I passed through their threadbare souls, unsure what had drawn Granny's spirit back to the place, but desperate to follow wherever she led. As I drew close, she ascended the stairs, and I followed, grabbing the railing tight and lurching up each step like the broken creature I was. Upstairs, I followed Granny into my bedroom, where Lady Pecan Tree continued her constant vigil at the window. The sheets were pulled back on the bed, and I knew that's where I belonged.

I lay down, and Granny tucked me in.

I desperately wanted to delve into the mystery of why she had come. Was part of Granny still in that other place, and this was indeed just another aspect of her soul? Or was I dead now myself, and she'd come to welcome me to the afterlife? But as these thoughts raced through my head, the pain stampeded through my body, and I could do nothing but writhe and moan beneath the covers.

Granny sat down, and I felt the bed sink beneath her.

Everything's going to be okay.

She wasn't speaking, but I could understand her.

I was right. This isn't a bad place.

Maybe she meant the house. Maybe she meant the afterlife. I reached out, tried to pull her in close, but she drifted away toward the ceiling.

Gave you a gift once. Time for you to pass it along.

And then she was gone.

Sadness collapsed over top of me, and I realized I was wailing in my bed. Overcome by grief. Overcome by pain.

Shirley abandoned her party, sat in the chair beside my bed all night. Watched me toss and turn and scream.

Next morning I woke, lonelier than I'd ever felt.

But not dead. Not quite yet.

———

There was a pond on the north end of town where kids used to go fishing for perch. I'd bathe in that brown water every couple of days, and I did so that morning, while I still had strength to wander. The water was warm, and it felt nice to luxuriate there for a time beneath the endless blue skies. My pain was dull and distant. I felt momentarily alive. Afterward, I drip-dried beneath the blazing sun, put on my clothes, then walked up the street toward the town square. In an alley between the café and the pharmacy, I found an abandoned bicycle that appeared almost new. A candy-red Haro that looked like it came off a BMX poster from my childhood. My legs were too long, and my back too stiff, but I raced that thing around town regardless, laughing, hopping curbs with only a minimum of damage to my pride and my shinbones.

Eventually I pedaled back to Granny's house and parked the bike in the yard. Beverly was sitting on the porch waiting for me with a grin on her face.

"Not bad for a broke-down old man," she said.

"Yeah, I have my days."

Already I felt my body growing stiffer and the pain swelling up in my gut, but riding that bike around was worth it. Granny's spectral visit had revitalized me, at least for a time, so I managed to hide my discomfort and greet Beverly with a hug.

"Hoyle had to work. Says to tell you howdy." Beverly held up a brown paper sack soaked with grease. "Wanted me to bring you these. You hungry?"

"Today I am."

Beverly's husband, Hoyle, had joined one of her early visits here, ostensibly to help carry in groceries, but like as not he wanted to put eyes on me, make sure his wife wasn't being charmed by a serial killer. Hard to blame him. Hoyle drove an F250 pickup truck with the logo for an oil field supply company on the door, and he buttoned his long-sleeve shirts all the way to the wrists, even in the dead of summer. He wore a straw cowboy hat and down-at-heel Tony Lamas. His sunburned face was friendly and furrowed with deep wrinkles. One look at me was enough to determine I was no harm to anyone, except for myself. The two of us got on well enough, and I was happy to see him on the occasions that he joined Beverly for a visit. Though he did have a harder time hiding his pity than Beverly did, and that wore on me sometimes.

We stepped into the house, and Willie sang *"Last Thing I Needed First Thing This Morning."* We sat at the kitchen table, and Beverly revealed the contents of the bag. Fried burritos from the filling station. A West Texas delicacy. We squirted packets of taco sauce on the burritos and went to town. In that moment, bathing in the glory of my cycling exploits and my temporary reprieve from crippling pain, life felt like something worth holding on to. Even Shirley looked longingly at those burritos, like she might be trying to recall what her favorite food used to be.

"You feeling all right?" said Beverly. "I wouldn't have imagined you spry enough for a bike ride."

"Last night was rough. Today's a little better."

"Wasn't sure where you were when I got here. I was afraid for a minute you might have finally floated off into the sky."

Beverly was joking, but it was a stinging reminder that everything I'd tried hadn't worked yet, and she still didn't entirely believe in what I was doing.

I gobbled up the rest of my food, pushed back in my chair, and lit a cigarette. Who could blame her? Can you really miss someone so much you're able to bridge the gap between life and death?

I believed it, but no longer expected anyone else to.

Beverly pulled a couple of bottles of Dr. Pepper from her bag, still mostly cold. "Hoyle sent these along too."

"Tell Hoyle he's a saint."

"You know I wouldn't be much of a friend if I didn't ask you again, can't we get you to a hospital where you'll be more comfortable? If it's about insurance, we're happy to help."

"You know it's not about insurance," I said.

"I have to be straight with you," she said. "You look half dead already. I'm sorry. I know that's cruel. But your morning escapade aside, you're in no shape to take care of yourself here anymore."

"I'll be fine, Beverly. I'm going to die either way."

"Maybe I don't want you to die out here all alone."

Beverly had tears in her eyes, and I felt suddenly ashamed. I suppose I'd not considered that someone might be that concerned about me. Might mourn when

I died, or if I left the world through other means. And no doubt she'd suffered her own share of grief when Granny vanished. They'd been close, and Beverly had no belief in the supernatural to comfort her. Not even garden-variety religion.

Surely it was selfishness alone that had caused me to drag her into this again.

But it was far too late for me to plot a better course now.

"I'm sorry," I said. "But I'm staying here."

"You're dying," she said. "How can you be so calm?"

"Because I *want* this. I've always wanted this."

"Explain it to me again," she said. "Tell it like I'm someone who won't think you're crazy. Like I'm your best friend in the world."

That summoned a mirthless smile to my face. Beverly *was* my best friend in the world, whether she knew it or not.

My earlier exertion caught up with me, and I felt exhaustion tunneling through my bloodstream, slowing my body to a crawl. The heat was murderous, and I put the cold Dr. Pepper bottle against my temple, tried to steady my breathing. The burritos churned in my chest, threatened to reappear, and the room spun around me like a spring tornado. I took steady hold of the table, struggled to gather my faculties so Beverly would have no further excuse to rush me off to a hospital. Smiled. Sipped at the soda. Spoke slowly, my voice dry as a sandstorm.

"Wherever Granny went, that's where I'm going."

"And to get there, you're casting a spell."

"Yep. It's already been cast, really. Right now, I'm just riding it like a runaway bull. Things are getting strange around here, Beverly. I know you can't feel what's happening, but please believe me."

"How long until the portal opens?"

How long until you die, is what she wanted to ask, but she was trying to meet me halfway.

"Could happen any time. A month from now, or today, while you and me are sitting here at the table. Which reminds me, I have a present for you."

"Brady, I don't need presents."

"You need this one."

I struggled to my feet, moved slow as a sloth across the kitchen floor, waved Beverly off as she tried to help me along. Whatever energy I'd borrowed from the universe that morning had been reclaimed.

In the living room, we sat on the creaky old couch while I dug through one of the cardboard boxes I'd brought in from the car. From within, I produced the amulet Granny had gifted me, and I handed it to Beverly.

"Here it is," I said. "*Safeheart.*"

"I certainly can't take a necklace from you."

"You don't believe any of this," I said. "And that's okay. But indulge my insanity. Don't think of this as a necklace, think of it as *protection.* Put it on, and please don't come around here anymore unless you're wearing it. Granny gave this to me, and I didn't understand why. But I figured it out. *Safeheart* will keep you grounded to the earth if you happen to be here when the portal opens. I would rather you be far away when that happens, but I'm too selfish to ask you to stay away entirely. So please wear it. No matter what."

Beverly examined the talisman for a bit, then put the chain around her neck. "I guess I don't mind wearing it, if it makes you feel better."

"It does."

Safeheart hung heavy against Beverly's chest. Gave me a sense of peace.

Gave you a gift once. Time for you to pass it along.

Past time, to tell the truth. There was no controlling the portal at this point. No stopping the metaphysical machine. I wondered if Granny had felt a similar sort of helplessness as everything she'd set in motion approached its inevitable end.

"Your grandmother told you this would keep you safe?"

"Yeah, she did," I said.

"Well, seems she was right," said Beverly. "You're the only one who didn't disappear."

"She was right about a whole lot of things."

Beverly placed her hand over the face of the amulet, smiled broadly like she was drawing sweet memories from the heart of the stone. "My favorite story your grandmother told was that one about a ghost named Jim."

"I never heard her tell that one," I said. "And it's not in any of her books."

"Yeah? Maybe she didn't write it down."

Beverly closed her eyes, hand still on her chest, *Safeheart* in her grip. I understood the power of that amulet. The sensation. And I could sense her drawing marginally closer to the strangeness she'd forever desired, but had always been too afraid to embrace.

"This was up near Lubbock, I think," she said. "Family up there had a ghost they called Jim, and they talked with him using a homemade Ouija board. Jim claimed to be nine hundred years old, and couldn't spell worth a lick, but he *knew* things. Whatever questions the family had, they'd ask Jim, and usually he was spot-on. Where are the car keys? Will the weather be okay for the football game Friday night, or is it gonna rain? Jim was always happy to help, so long as they turned on the television programs he liked after. That always made me laugh when she told it. A ghost watching television.

"One day the oldest son in the house drove to Dallas for a school trip. The parents asked Jim to confirm he'd made it there safely, but straight away the Ouija board came to life and Jim spelled out "Austin" and "girl" and they knew then the boy had lied about his trip. Jim was accommodating enough to provide the name of the hotel in Austin, and the room number where the son was staying with his girlfriend—and when the parents called, sure enough, he answered. Jim got an extra hour of television that night."

"I can't believe she never told me that one," I said.

"She had a million of them, Brady."

"I wonder if Jim is still there."

"Maybe," she said. "Jim apparently loved being part of their family. Told them that place was his home."

"You coming to visit again in a few days?" I asked.

"Of course."

A small part of me actually hoped I'd still be here when she did.

I'd spent a lifetime trying to vanish from the world, only to find a real home at the end of all things.

Summer had one foot in the grave when the portal finally claimed me. This reckoning arrived at high noon; my last stand against the insistency of life occurred beneath a relentless yellow sun that burned away all the color from the world and left it begging for autumn. Sleep had been fitful. I'd spent half the night screaming, coughing up bits of my lungs. But by late morning, I managed to sit up, put my bare feet on the bedroom floor, and embrace the wonder of my last moments on earth.

The air resonated with an otherworldly power. Static tugged at the bedsheets and lifted the hair on my arms. With effort, I stood. Moved slowly across the room, biting back the pain, and listening to the low thrumming noise that enveloped the house.

There was *music* in that sound.

I knew in my heart and my blood and my bones that the day had arrived.

Lady Pecan Tree was unmoved by unfolding events. She remained at her window, and I joined her there, eager to watch the portal eye open overhead and meet its gaze. Reality *shuddered*. Became threadbare. When I reached the window, I leaned close to the glass, inadvertently stumbled, and found myself inhabiting Lady Pecan Tree's space. The veil between the living and the dead, in those last moments, was razor-thin. And so, before I could move away and apologize, I took up residence in her soul. Together we looked out the dormer window, saw the town as it had been long ago. Horses lashed to posts in front of the mercantile. Wagons cutting ruts through dusty streets. Wind raced in from the west, rattled the branches of a towering pecan tree occupying the space where a church would one day stand. Sand rode the currents, clattered against the windows of the land office and the drinking parlor.

Lady Pecan Tree directed our gaze downward to the yard. No picket fencing. No grass. Just a few head of cattle being herded through the streets by sunburned men on horseback, everyone moving slow as syrup from a tap in the terrible heat. A little girl stood in the shadows of the house, wearing a blue calico dress, hair a swarm of golden curls. She drew close to the cattle, hands reaching out to pet their soft hides as they passed. Her touch, a daily ritual. But this day, a longhorn startled. Trampled the little girl beneath its hooves in the span of a heartbeat. Screaming filled the air, and one of the cowboys slid from his saddle and rushed to help. The angry animal turned, lashed out with one of its long horns, shattered the man's skull, and tore away half the skin from his face. Eventually the other riders calmed the creature, separated it from the herd, but it was too late for the girl. The injured cowboy crawled away, howling, but somehow alive. Lady Pecan Tree lifted our gaze again, and we saw the faceless man hanging from the huge pecan tree in the center of town, felled by despair. Boots a foot off the ground, body tossed about by the relentless wind.

Grief flowed through me like an electrical charge, and I let myself fall away from Lady Pecan Tree. When I sloughed off her ghost, it felt like shedding a suit of uncomfortable clothes.

I lay panting on the ground, tears in my eyes and a wail in my throat. A fleet of ghost hands grabbed my arms, helped me stand. Ten ghosts, a dozen, Shirley chief among them. They ushered me from Lady Pecan Tree's shadow before her grief could swallow me whole. The Lady still wouldn't acknowledge me, but the gravity of her mourning threatened to pull me back into her mind, to pin me to the earth alongside her, for an eternity of regret. For the first time I understood what might lead a person to surrender themselves to the material world entirely, and having done so, how inextricably they bound their souls to the past. But it wasn't tragedy that threatened to capture and keep me, it was love. It was friendship. These things I'd never had much experience with now threatened to derail my plan.

"Please," I said. "Help me get downstairs."

The ghosts half carried me down the stairs and to the already-open door.

When I walked out onto the porch, they remained inside, gathered at the threshold. Shirley cried silvery tears; I'd promised to leave some part of me behind to keep her company, but I'm not sure she believed me. The noonday skies darkened, and I realized my time was now. Shirley reached out her arms. I knelt to receive her fierce hug. When I pulled away and stood, we were both crying, but resolute. She shooed me away, trying her best to smile. Music came rushing from the house like a river overrunning its banks, loud enough to set me in motion. No mournful songs this time. Willie sang "I'll Fly Away," the old gospel song. I couldn't help but laugh, and sing along. The joyful music propelled me across the porch and down the cedar steps.

My pain forgotten.

My heart aching with anticipation.

Like Granny before me, I lifted my eyes to the sky to greet the afterlife.

The portal inhaled the world. Lifted me into the air. Blue light pulsed brighter than creation. Music resonated through my bones. Ice-cold wind stirred the air around me and tore at my clothes. As I rose higher, I spotted someone rushing up the street toward the house. Beverly. She reached the picket fence, let a sack of groceries fall to the ground as she watched my skyward progress. Apples and oranges rolled down the sidewalk. Beverly waved her arms, screamed something I couldn't hear. Longing welled up so fast inside me, it felt like a knot in my throat, but there was no turning back now. The portal roared, and the music grew louder. The wind battered the old house and scattered the porch chairs into the yard. Beverly grabbed onto the fence railing as the storm threatened to knock her over. *Safeheart* hung around her neck. Likely an afterthought when she'd dressed that morning, but now the only thing keeping her from flying away. She was crying, still trying to scream for me. The blue light was blinding, but I could still make out the terror in her expression.

The *truth* seared into her eyes.

Would people believe her when she told this story?

God, I hoped so.

The portal pulled me higher, until I could see the house far below and the unforgiving West Texas landscape stretching forever in all directions.

I closed my eyes. My friends were out of sight, and there was nothing else left I wanted to see in the world.

Eventually the storm relented. The light grew soft.

Only the music remained.

So, I opened my eyes, gazed upon the mystery.

And it was everything I'd always dreamed it would be.

CODA:
THE AFTERLIFE OF A HOME

There's a town in West Texas where nobody lives.

More of a graveyard than a town anymore. Memories gone cold and gray. Everybody recalls somebody who used to live there, all those years ago, but nobody remembers exactly who they were, or what happened to them. Maybe they joined a UFO cult. Maybe the Lord lifted them up to glory. Maybe a hole opened in the sky and swallowed them in one hungry gulp.

Whatever. It's a strange place.

Now it's become the realm of teenagers. No adult wants to think about how terrifying and unpredictable the universe can be. They don't want to consider a town where the population simply vanished, let alone invest their lives and their money into rebuilding such a cursed place. Children would swarm there in search of whimsy and ghosts if they only had the means. But the town is fixed deep in the parched desert, far beyond the reach of bicycles and skateboards.

But teenagers with their sudden access to cars? Teenagers looking for a place to drink and smoke and search for trouble? Yeah, this is their spot.

They alone stalk these streets, too alive with laughter. Hot blood in their young veins. As far from death as they will ever be again, and yet closer than they think. They heft rocks at windows and shake spray paint cans so that the metallic clatter echoes through the collapsing buildings. They color the windows and the bricks with their angst. They toss the cans in the streets and seek out the shadows. They kiss in the darkness. They taste the night and surrender to its dangerous call.

Bonfires burn in the middle of the downtown intersection, a long-dead stoplight sagging overhead. Boots stomp beer cans flat. Whisky bottles take flight and crash against the old, decaying church. This town is a carnival. A place for dark exploration. Nobody will find them here, and there are no rules to follow.

Well, maybe there's one.

Not any sort of official rule. Just a truth that lives in the young guts of every wild teen who visits this place.

The town is your playground. But don't mess with the ghost house.

It stands a block off the square, window eyes covered in cataracts of dust, but still able to watch the reluctant approach of all those who dare. Nobody targets this place with their .22 rifles or their spray paint. Nobody even ventures past the leaning picket fence and into the tidy front yard.

But you can hear the music from the street. And some small few can see the ghosts.

A little girl. A little boy. Peering out from the windows. Sometimes their arms are loaded with books. Other times, they hold hands, silently singing old country songs. The music is quiet and mournful. But their eyes are alive and smiling; these children know you're here.

They see you. They watch.

And you understand, deep in your bones, that if you pushed through the front gate, made your way up onto the porch and crossed the threshold, you'd never walk out again. You'd join those ghosts in their forever.

And standing there, in front of that house? Well, maybe that's not such a bad thing.

More than one person has remained there too long, letting that haunted place resonate around them, and considered leaving their whole lives behind. People say lights splash overhead. The sky boils and screams. Stand there long enough, and everyone you love, everyone you lost, will find you.

Close your eyes. Listen to that sad music. Wait for the dead to embrace you.

Whether you stay with them or not is entirely up to you.

AFTERWORD

My grandmother was a paranormal researcher.

This was in the late seventies, early eighties. Long before the proliferation of ghost hunting television shows. The occult was having a heyday though—ancient aliens and UFOs and bigfoot all took center stage in our weirdo consciousness, and as a child, I became absorbed in all that cool stuff and more, largely due to my grandmother.

She was the ghost lady. Known in our region of West Texas as the person to come to with your stories of the strange and the supernatural. She wasn't always that way, but she came to her calling in middle age, and once she did, there was no turning back.

Her bookshelves were filled with titles like *The Amityville Horror* and *Chariots of the Gods*. Books about pyramid power, and crystal skulls, and alien abductions. Greek mythology and world folklore of all kinds. Not to mention Ray Bradbury books and story collections like *Alfred Hitchcock Presents: Stories Not for the Nervous*. These books drew me in with their dark allure.

They still do.

All these things informed the writer I became, and all the weird stuff I create. Like the book you've just read.

Once word spread about my grandmother's interest in the supernatural, her collection of stories and photographs grew in a hurry. She had stacks of cassettes with interviews, ghostly sounds, and all manner of creepy paraphernalia, along with stacks of research on regional ghost tales. It was her hope to one day write a book about West Texas ghosts, but she passed away when I was a teenager, and never had the chance.

A lot of her ghost stuff is still around. A lot of it is in a box in my closet.

This novella is purely fiction. But many of the memories are real. The stories told in the narrative here are all stories someone told my grandmother. Stories from her files. That includes the photograph that changes. I have the original. I have several copies.

And yes, last time I checked, new things had appeared.

I don't have an answer for how that happens. I don't have an explanation for any of my grandmother's stories.

But I believe every one of them.

Whether they're true or not, doesn't really matter.

ACKNOWLEDGMENTS

Thanks to Sean Markey, E. Catherine Tobler, and all the folks at Psychopomp/The Deadlands. That magazine has inspired me to write a lot of recent fiction that might otherwise have gone unwritten, and I'm grateful my work has found a home there. When I read that Psychopomp was opening to novella submissions, I was determined to write something that aimed right at the heart of what The Deadlands is all about. At least to me. *Summer in the House of the Departed* is the result, and I'm so happy I didn't miss my shot.

Thanks to a few kind folks who read this story prior to submission, to help make sure I hadn't gone entirely off the rails. C.S. Humble, Ryan Leslie, and Chris Panatier. All three fantastic writers and even better humans. Keep it up, y'all.

Thanks to my agent, Kris O'Higgins for doing the hard stuff.

Thanks to my wife, Kristin, for being my favorite person ever.

And thanks to the many booksellers, reviewers, readers, librarians, and other awesome souls in the writing community who have embraced my books and come back for more. There's a lot of my blood in this book, but my heart's in there too. Really hope you dig it.

www.ingramcontent.com/pod-product-compliance
Lightning Source LLC
Chambersburg PA
CBHW030010010826
48973CB00009B/2740